P9-DBJ-871

THE PIGMAN'S LEGACY

Paul Zindel

BANTAM BOOKS
NEW YORK • TORONTO • LONDON • SYDNEY • AUCKLAND

RL 6, IL age 12 and up

THE PIGMAN'S LEGACY

A Bantam Book / published by arrangement with
Harper & Row, Publishers, Inc.

PUBLISHING HISTORY

Harper & Row edition published September 1980
Serialized in Scholastic Voice, September 1980

Bantam edition / October 1981
8 printings through November 1988

The Starfire logo is a registered trademark of Bantam Books, a division of
Bantam Doubleday Dell Publishing Group, Inc. Registered in U.S. Patent and
Trademark Office and elsewhere.

ISBN 0-553-26599-7

Bantam Books are published by Bantam Books, a division of Bantam
Doubleday Dell Publishing Group, Inc. Its trademark, consisting of the
words "Bantam Books" and the portrayal of a rooster, is Registered in
U.S. Patent and Trademark Office and in other countries. Marca Regis-
trada. Bantam Books, 1540 Broadway, New York, New York 10036.

PRINTED IN THE UNITED STATES OF AMERICA

OPM   30   29

A *New York Times*
Notable Children's Book

THE PIGMAN'S LEGACY

"The Zindel style that makes you laugh through tears results in frenzied adventures, enthralling examples of four people armed by love, forcing hard luck to say 'uncle.' "
—*Publishers Weekly*

"The author has made use of contemporary jargon, quirky characters, and bizarre situations to uncover a fundamentally human meaning lurking beneath the madness."
—*The Horn Book Magazine*

"John and Lorraine have mellowed and matured a little . . . but more importantly, they have learned a lot about caring for others."
—*School Library Journal*

Paul Zindel is the award-winning author of many books for young people including THE PIGMAN; MY DARLING, MY HAMBURGER; I NEVER LOVED YOUR MIND; A STAR FOR THE LATE-COMER (with Bonnie Zindel); and the Pulitzer Prize-winning play, *The Effect of Gamma Rays on Man-in-the-Moon Marigolds*.

The Promise

We, the undersigned kids, make this solemn promise to tell the truth and nothing but the truth, and we pray that anyone who reads this won't go around saying the terrible things they said about us and the first old man who became our friend. His name was the Pigman and certain persons who read that memorial epic said we knocked him off. Please don't believe them. We didn't kill the Pigman. We never even meant to hurt him. But we can't be phonies. We, the undersigned kids, are scared that you're going to blame us for still another death, but we've got to tell the story anyway. We're typing this one in the third-floor book closet at Franklin High with a portable Smith-Corona typewriter sitting on a stack of *Hamlet*s. We are going to tell you everything the way it happened and we just hope that the rest of you kids learn from our mistakes. Signed with imitation blood borrowed permanently from the Acting Club,

John Conlan

Lorraine Jensen

The
Pigman's
Legacy

One

In case you didn't read the first memorial epic Lorraine and I wrote about the Pigman, don't worry about it. I never used to like reading either because a lot of my teachers made me read stuff I didn't need. I may be retarded and selfish but I only like to read things that are going to help me in *my* life. I mean Lady Macbeth says a lot of brilliant things, but Shakespeare or no Shakespeare, I don't know what she's talking about, and I'm not a stupid boy. Maybe someday I'll be ready for characters like her and Coriolanus and that girl who had to wear the scarlet letter. But right now I find them so boring I could barf. In fact, whenever my English teachers tell me I have to read a book and write a book report about it, I go straight to the library and look for the thinnest book on the shelf. Consequently I have given book reports on such subjects as the tulips of Alaska, Peruvian baseball, and the poetry of Rimbaud—a wild boy who croaked so young he didn't have time to write all that much. Also, nobody calls me the Bathroom Bomber at all anymore because it's been ages since I gave up setting off firecrackers in the boys' john. The only practical jokes I do now are those designed to show the warm foibles of being human. Like a couple of months ago I tied the end of a catgut line from my fishing reel to one of Lorraine's old pocketbooks and left it around for kids to rip off. When somebody would pick it up, I'd let them get about a hundred yards before I'd start reeling them in and you should have seen the surprised looks on their faces when I snapped them around. Also, I've given up writing graffiti on desks. The few times I've had to write graffiti at all lately I've done it on a neat 3 x 5 card and Scotch-taped it to someone's back. Like:

Keep America Clean—
EAT A Pigeon

Also you should know I now don't condone the marking and destruction of public property. Whenever I see these subway trains and buses with Magic Marker writing and spray-can painting on them, I'd like to get whoever did it and immerse them in a vat of two-hundred-year-old wonton soup. And then I'd like to catch all the night watchmen and inspectors who are supposed to protect our trains and buses because they are not doing their jobs. They're probably goofing off in little shacks drinking beer and having smokes, which is why some demented delinquent can sneak in to write in thick eight-foot-tall blue Day-Glow letters NORTON WAS HERE on the entire side of seventy-six Staten Island Rapid Transit local train cars.

The one shady thing I still do is curse. But Lorraine, the traditionalist that she is, still won't let me curse in our second memorial epic. If I want to write a curse it has to be the old system of @#$% for a mild curse and 3@#$% for a horrendous curse. Maybe because the world is so awful just now is the reason everybody's going around saying @#$% on you and go 3@#$% yourself all the time. I don't know.

Also, almost everything that happens in our bizarre escapade that you're about to read, provided you're not hauled off to a loony bin before you finish the epic, is haunted by this dead man called the Pigman. And you don't really have to know exactly who the Pigman was in order to understand the strange things that happened after he shuffled off this mortal coil. All you have to do is understand a little about what it's like to feel guilty about something. And if you've never felt guilty about anything then you must be a lily-white angel from heaven, in which case you really should stop reading this immediately before you have celestial cardiac arrest.

Lorraine is already panting to get at the typewriter, and since she's the kind of pubescent expert on psychology we need at this point, it's just as well.

Two

As usual, I should never have let John write the first chapter. I am not a pubescent expert on anything. I simply happen to like psychology and read a lot of books on the subject. I happen to think that kids and everyone can find salvation through Freud, Jung, and a few other great minds of our century. And I'm sorry John doesn't like reading about them or Lady Macbeth, but I happen to think they've got a few things to teach us. I'll admit I too don't know what Lady Macbeth talks about whenever we have to read that play, which seems to be just about every year. Let's just say I know enough about guilt trips to know that they're not vacations, but what John and I are really trying to tell you is that you don't have to know a whole lot about our past in order to understand what we're going to tell you. All you have to know is that once upon a time we were a little younger and met a sweet lonely old man who tried to be a kid again but died. He lived in an old house on Howard Avenue and he used to give us a lot of presents and let us sip some wine with him now and then. I'll even have you know that there are some people who think that we gave *him* things too. Some people said we weren't fleecing him and that we weren't responsible for his death. Some say the best present we ever gave him was our youth. And if you ask me I think Freud, Jung, and even Harry Stack Sullivan would have approved of the entire relationship. It's only the mean people who say the gift we gave him was death. And to those people we could be just as mean back to them and say it was the Pigman who killed our childhood. And to be truthful, neither John nor I was really sure who was right, which I suppose is the real reason we've got to tell you what happened after the Pigman went to his grave.

4

I guess there does come a time in everybody's childhood when somebody does kill it. Every kid has his childhood die at some point. Maybe your childhood is already dead as you are reading this or maybe we're going to kill it, or maybe it's still alive and going to live on for a couple more years—but eventually it has to go to stiff city. I think that's what a Pigman really does even if he doesn't mean to. If you are a kid and somebody has already killed your childhood then you know what I'm talking about. A Pigman is anybody who comes into your life and causes a voice inside of you to say, "Okay buster, the jig's up. There's no more Santa Claus. There's no more Easter Rabbit. There's no more blaming Mommy or Daddy or your teachers or your brothers or your sisters or your friends, *there's only you!*" And the day your childhood dies is probably the first day you really know what guilt is. When your childhood dies it's so painful you figure you must have done something absolutely dreadful to be left hurting so badly inside. You want to lock yourself in your room and hide in your closet and scream. One kid I know had a mother who got killed in a car crash and he knew what I was talking about. Even if it's a divorce, if your father or mother walks out, that can make you feel like you've met a Pigman. If your dog gets run over and you didn't have it on a leash. If your cat gets distemper because you didn't give it all the right shots. These are all like encounters with a Pigman. Even though the Pigman himself could be a wonderful person. They don't mean to kill your childhood, it just works out that way. Somehow a Pigman makes you grow up and so it's for you who have met a Pigman, or even more, I suppose, for those who hear the footsteps of a Pigman coming near, that John and I must write this epic. We've already met our Pigman and can now tell you how we found out whether the legacy he left us was the legacy of life or the legacy of death.

It was last May, about four months after our Pigman died, that John and I were riding home platonically as usual after school, and we got so involved in a discussion on the therapeutic value of mourning that we'd gone two bus stops past our regular stop before we remembered to get off. I had been talking about how important it is to cry when somebody dies, and John said you really didn't have to cry *outside*, you could cry *inside*. And I told him that sublimation was just as dangerous as anything else the human mind could do, but I didn't mind having to walk farther than usual because I liked walking alone with John—even though I didn't know if he really liked walking alone with me. We weren't a romantic item, but ever since the Pigman's death whenever we walked alone John would hold my hand. You might as well know here that sometimes I could feel electricity flowing through my fingers into his, which wasn't amazing, since we'd both turned sixteen and John still has long brown hair and gigantic eyes that can not only look right through you but grab your heart while they're doing it. Anyway, we were just walking along and after about five minutes John and I noticed something very peculiar. Without realizing it we had started strolling along Howard Avenue, and we were walking right toward Mr. Pignati's old house. Mr. Pignati was our Pigman's real name, and somehow we had always tried to avoid that particular route to get home ever since he had died.

"I don't like what I'm feeling," I told John.

"What's that?"

"*Anxiety.*"

John held my hand tighter. "We can go back the other way," he said.

"No, that'll take too long."

But as soon as I said that, I felt a cold wind sweep between us and I began to shiver. Goose pimples rose up out of my skin like a million tiny icebergs. We started to walk around a bend past all the old villas that once housed the elite of Staten Island, when we heard a *whirring* sound in the air. It was chilling, like a continual shriek coming from the outer reaches of the universe. I even thought John could see the thump of my heart right through my sweater, because he squeezed my hand so hard I thought he was going to cut off the circulation in my fingers. I didn't need anyone to draw me a picture to know that John was a little frightened too, because ever since the Pigman had died his nerves

6

seemed to have been on edge. I think what was happening to us was that we truly expected to see the ghost of our dead friend come swirling toward us.

It wasn't until we had completely rounded the bend that we became certain that the whirring sound was coming right in our direction. Suddenly we saw what it was. A little old nun was sitting on top of a small tractor mower, cutting the grass in front of the Grymes Hill Convent there.

John and I looked at each other in disbelief, and burst into laughter. If I hadn't known better I would've thought John had set this whole thing up just to scare me. We did the best we could to muffle our giggles because we didn't want the nun to think we were laughing at her even though she was a bit of a sight sitting atop that tractor with her habit and the chopped grass undulating in the air behind her. It wasn't until she turned up the convent's driveway that John and I could really compose ourselves. Some psychologists would simply say our laughter was a type of nervous release, but in just a few steps more we were standing right in front of the Pigman's old house, 190 Howard Avenue. The house had changed a great deal since we had last seen it. Its simple wooden frame looked as though some terrible witch had put a curse upon it and sentenced it to sleep for a hundred years. The bushes had grown so wild the house was submerged in a jungle of vines and thorns.

"Look over there, Lorraine."

I almost wanted to cry. A large limb from the huge maple tree on the side of the house had split in half and was just hanging. The rest of the tree was covered with leaves, but this limb was dead, and no one had ever taken it down. That was what hurt the most—that it was clear no one cared about this house anymore. It had no doubt been left to rot and just wait for some real-estate speculators and bulldozers who would more than likely come one day and demolish it.

"I feel terrible," I said. "I feel as if someone's telling us to take all our wonderful memories of the fun we had in this house and bury them with Mr. Pignati."

"I know," John said softly.

7

We just stood there, hypnotized by the house, remembering the past. Then the wind started to blow again. Suddenly I was talking to myself. *What was that? What is that curtain flapping at the window upstairs? What am I seeing? What is that moving? My eyes must be playing tricks on me!* There was a face in the window. Dark, ominous eyes staring out into the street at me—and I knew they could see my eyes staring back.

I reached my hand to my mouth to muffle a scream, and the face disappeared.

"John! did you see that?" I asked as my blood froze and my mouth dropped open.

Three

I didn't see what Lorraine was talking about. In fact the only reason I think she had ghosts on the brain was because of all those psychology books she reads. I tried to tell her that all psychologists are screwballs, which is why they go into the field anyway.

"No, I didn't see anything," I told Lorraine. But I'm afraid I said it a little too quickly. I suppose the truth of the matter was that I wasn't sure. Maybe there was something, but it was probably a *reflection* from something. It could have been a shadow from the berserk foliage around the old house. But with Lorraine and her built-in radar equipment I sometimes have to listen to her because you can never tell what signals she's picking up on. The month before, Lorraine had the same dream three nights in a row. I mean that's the kind of psychology freak she is. She said in this dream she was walking down the main aisle in the school cafeteria and kept seeing some person with flashlights for ears. Now ordinarily that would just seem very crazy, but the very next week this lady by the name of Dolly Racinski was hired as the cafeteria-floor sweeper. It was sad to see this happy and perky little sixtyish old woman pushing a broom and picking up squashed half-pint milk containers, which all the teenage baboons jump on so they make explosion sounds. But the really weird part was that Dolly Racinski wore giant-sized pom-pom-shaped rhinestone earrings that sparkled exactly as if she was wearing flashlights in her ears. And then whenever she took off the custodial smock, she always had on a green or gold electric-colored dress that was so bright you'd think she was on fire. She pushed that broom and her earrings would swing from left to right—and we soon learned she never took her earrings off. It was just like that lady I read about once in the *National Enquirer* who was out in the rain and got struck by lightning which melted her left earring to her ear in such a way that she would have to wear it for life unless she wanted to have her ear cut off. It was funny how Lorraine and I thought of her dream the moment we saw Dolly. In fact it was spooky considering the fact that Dolly would one day come to play such an important part in our lives. Of course we're the ones who made her play that part, because even from the first day she came to work we used to say, "Hi, Dolly. How are you feeling today?" She'd push the broom by and say, "Lookin' up! Lookin' up!" And sometimes when other kids would throw pennies and M&M's at her, we'd yell at them. And she would come over to us and say, "You kids are swell. You kids are just *swell.*"

But at the moment Lorraine saw the ghost on Howard Avenue we really didn't think Dolly Racinski or anybody was going to help us. Of course, we are very used to not getting help from the adult world at all, as a general rule.

"It was a ghost," Lorraine insisted as she rushed down the street fleeing the old house.

"There are no such things as ghosts," I kept repeating, trotting in order to keep up with her.

"Oh come off it. You saw the eyes. They looked just like Mr. Pignati's."

"I didn't see any eyes."

"Yes you did.

"Mr. Pignati must have come back from the other side to give us a message," she said. "Dead people do things like that. I know about it!"

Lorraine babbled on a mile a minute all the way until we reached her house. She started quoting all these weird cases, like the time some famous poetess died and all her relatives saw this apparition rise up off her body and dance on the ceiling. And she told me it's a well-known fact that many star ghosts from Forest Lawn come out at night and run around that fancy cemetery— like Jean Harlow and Jeanette MacDonald have been seen prancing around the Hall of the Resurrection they have there. I tried to change the subject three times, but I couldn't stop her from talking about Duke University and all those other places that have experiments that prove the existence of supernatural presences and other spooks.

In front of Lorraine's house a very earthly presence made itself known to us.

"*Get in here*, Lorraine," her mother brayed from the front door. Now I don't want to be rude or anything, and in fact Lorraine and I decided we're not going to talk about parents a whole lot in this epic at all, but I'd rather be attacked by an alien from outer space than by Mrs. Jensen. I gave Lorraine's hand an extra squeeze and watched her disappear inside her house while Mrs. Jensen lingered a moment longer giving me what looked like the evil eye.

"*Good-bye*, John," Mrs. Jensen instructed in case I didn't know what to do.

Actually I didn't mind. Lorraine and I lately have begun to really understand our parents, so we don't ridicule them all that much anymore or pin the rap on them for everything that goes wrong. For the most part they leave us alone now that we've mellowed as high-school sophomores. The facts are still about the same though. Lorraine's mother is still a widow and a practical nurse who steals things like Lipton Cup•a•Soup and skinless sardines from houses where she works, and my mother, who is formally known as Mrs. Conlan, is informally known by me as the Old Lady and she's still an antiseptic freak who dashes around the house with a spray can of Lysol and tries occasionally to encase me in vinyl. I think that's about all the hereditary facts you've got to know or be reminded of except for the fact that my father is continuing his performance as a prime candidate for a heart attack working at the New York Coffee Exchange. His conversation is still so stimulating I continue to call him Bore. But there has been some change. All our parents are reading adult self-help books. Lorraine told me her mother's into transactional analysis now. I hope she's printed up her own T-shirt that says I DESERVE LOVE on the front and something like HONK FOR A KISS on the back. My mother, the Old Lady, is reading some book which has to do with her right to say "no" without feeling guilty whenever

11

she gets an urge to run outside and lemon Pledge the sidewalk. And my father is rereading *How to Hate Vodka,* which is a book that shows Russian natives cooking potatoes, with worms and flies falling into the vats. But what I really think is terrific is that our parents understand Lorraine and me much better now that they realize they're just as much in transition as we are. It really takes the heat off us now that our parents, our teachers, and everybody knows that life is *all* adolescence.

And I suppose I might as well take the time now to let you know when Lorraine wrote that we weren't a romantic item, it wasn't because I don't like Lorraine. She finally lost a few pounds and wears a little mascara on her pretty green eyes so she looks like a young Shirley MacLaine on diet pills. She thinks I didn't notice that her charms were growing, but let me tell you that her charms are growing so big that all the boys in the sophomore class have noticed them. She's not exactly Dolly Parton or Raquel Welch yet, but I'd say she's on her way.

That night at the dinner table the Old Lady said to me, "You're very quiet tonight, John."

"Yes," I agreed.

"What's the matter?" Bore wanted to know.

"I'm sorry. I'm tired," I admitted and simply excused myself from the table.

"I'm worried about you," the Old Lady said. "You look a little jittery."

"I'm okay, Mom," I said. Then I took my plate out to the kitchen. Ever since the Pigman died and I started carrying my own dirty dishes out to the kitchen, I can't tell you how happy that makes my parents. If you ever want to really shock your parents, just start carrying your dirty dishes out to the sink. And if you really want them to freak out, wash your own dishes. They'll go nuts. While I was out there I decided to get a breath of fresh air and have a cigarette. So I took the kitchen garbage bag out with me. I found that saved me a lot of anguish and seemed to bring exceptional ecstasy to the Old Lady and Bore. For some reason they really adore me ejecting the refuse. But I *wasn't* saved the anguish of smoking one of the spinach cigarettes Lorraine had insisted I switch to in the hope that I would give up smoking. What she didn't know was that I had discovered the only cure for the taste of one of her spinach cigarettes was to smoke one of my own normal ones. In fact I usually arranged my pack so half of it was filled with the spinach ones and the other half with plain old Parliament cigarettes. Lorraine just didn't understand that sometimes a cigarette is the only thing that can give me a clear head when I've got to think. And that's what I needed that night. Lorraine *had* made me jittery. What if Mr. Pignati *was* trying to reach us from the grave? I don't really believe in any of that garbage, but my mind is open to anything. I really get a little wacko whenever I'm guilty. Like if I didn't do my homework for Miss Gale's English class, I keep thinking I see Miss Gale all over the place. If I look into the sky it's like Miss Gale is flying over getting ready to drop bird turds on my head. And another thing, our Pigman was one guy who would do something like come back from the grave to let us know he was still thinking about us. And if you think that sounds nuts, you just wait until you love somebody like your mother or father and they croak, and you'll see them popping up all over the place. When my grandmother died I used to see her sitting in her rocking chair for weeks afterward.

The next day after school, Lorraine and I were coming home together on the bus and I told her the most sensible path of action was that we should just go straight over to the Pigman's house and find out what was going on. Maybe it was just a curtain moving. Maybe there was an owl living on the second floor. Maybe chipmunks had taken over the house. It was no big deal.

"Lorraine, I think we should go over to the Pigman's house."

"*No.*"

"Look, there is only one way to solve this and that's to confront it. We'll go over there and you'll see there's no ghost. Ghosts don't exist."

"And what if they do?" Lorraine asked, her eyes wet and fearful.

"Well, then we'll write our story for some spicy newspaper and call it 'Ghost Mutilates Franklin High Teenagers.' "

"What if it *kills* us and we can't write the story?"

"It will be journalism's loss." And then I just let out a horse laugh as though it was all just the most preposterous thing I'd heard in my life. I took Lorraine's hand and dragged her off the bus, and if she felt any electricity shooting out of my fingers, she sure as heck didn't show it on her face. All I knew was that I wanted to get over there as quickly as I could and get this thing over with once and for all. If I had known then what was going to happen, I think I would have just cut out my tongue and gotten on a slow boat to China.

Four

All the way to the Pigman's house John kept saying we had nothing to be afraid of, but my whole body was vibrating with nerves. When animals or human beings find themselves in unusual situations usually their adrenaline starts to flow, and they call that the *flight or fight* syndrome. At the moment I was beginning to favor flight. Finally we were in front of Mr. Pignati's house again. This time the windows were lifeless.

"Let's get it over with," John said.

We climbed up the squeaky old steps to the porch and swayed near the edge waiting for some belligerent spirit to come rushing out of the house with an axe. The thought crossed my mind that maybe, if there was a ghost, it might just be a playful one. The kind they call poltergeists. Poltergeists are the kind of ghosts that are just supposed to do things like shake your hand wearing cold cream, or push a grapefruit in your face.

"Look," John said, "the door is *wide* open."

"It's only open a crack," I corrected.

"Same thing."

"John, we can't go in there."

"Why not?"

"We'll be trespassing."

"A mere technicality," John insisted.

I stayed near the edge of the porch as John pushed the door completely open. *Nothing.* We went inside. *Nothing.* I moved to follow him and walked straight into a cobweb. I felt I had just kissed a tarantula and let out a scream. John was at my side in a flash helping me wipe the thing out of my mouth, but I was so sorry that I had overreacted. Finally he took my hand again and together we moved back inside the house, leaving the door open for a quick escape.

John and I felt almost lost in the living room. It was

as though we had never been there before. Most of the Pigman's old furniture was gone, and even the wooden floors seemed to be faded.

"The house is dying," I said.

"Maybe it's just as well," John sighed.

"The wallpaper is still the same."

"No it's not," he said, pointing out a spot in the dining room where it cascaded to the floor.

"Maybe we could fix it."

"What's the point?"

Actually John was right. We'd only be fixing it up for a bunch of dust in the air. We couldn't turn the house into a shrine for the dead. Our Pigman wouldn't have wanted that.

We went through the rest of the downstairs area and checked inside all the closets and under the radiators. We invaded the room behind the long black curtains where Mr. Pignati had kept all his little glass and marble pigs. I'll never forget the first moment we saw Mr. Pignati's collection of strange motley pigs, and how they were all broken by a mean kid called Norton. Now the room was barren, and the memory was so painful I had to get out of there immediately.

"The refrigerator's running," John hollered from the kitchen.

"Go catch it," I called back, thinking John was joking just to lift my spirits.

"No, I'm serious," John blurted. "The light goes on when I open the refrigerator door. There's food in here."

I rushed into the kitchen.

"What is this?" John asked, taking out a carton from the refrigerator.

"Acidophilus milk," I read from the label.

"It sounds like a disease." John was getting a crazy excitement in his voice and I started to get nervous again. Something in the back of my mind told me that acidophilus milk might be one of those things my mother would use on a patient. I wasn't sure. Suddenly there was a sound from upstairs and a scraping noise that stopped as quickly as it started.

John's eyes rolled upward toward the ceiling. My heart started doing flip-flops.

"Let's check it out," John whispered, grabbing my hand.

We headed for the stairs cautiously. For some reason I thought of us as two little monkeys in a zoo clinging to each other as we started up the steps.

"Let's not and say we did," I said.

"We're going up," John insisted.

"One thing you don't want to do is run right up and scare off a ghost," I advised, hoping that he would have time to consider clearing out altogether.

John just continued moving me up the stairs. "Mr. Pignati's spirit is here," John said. "I can feel it. I really can."

My throat felt as though it was going to close. The capillaries in my head were like the strings on a piano pounding out some atonal etude. It was all so unscientific, I wanted to say. We should get notes. We should have oscilloscopes. We should have electrodes in our heads. We should be recording all this for *Psychology Today* or some other illustrious scientific journal. Instead I said nothing and allowed John to haul me up alongside him. At the top of the stairs, we could see into the bathroom. Everything looked okay there.

"It's the same old shower curtain," John pointed out. I watched him go in and open the medicine cabinet. Some shaving cream was in there. And for some bizarre reason John's face lit up at that discovery. "Someone *is* here," he said with an assurance that made my jaw petrify.

"Let's get out of here," I finally managed to utter.

"Mr. Pignati, are you there?" John began to speak to the air in front of him. "It's John and Lorraine," John called gently into the hallway leading to the Pigman's old bedroom.

The door to the room was closed, but the scraping sound from beyond reached my ears with no trouble at all.

"Did you hear that?" I asked John.

"Naw," John said, "it's nothing."

"Are you crazy? It sounds like the top of a coffin sliding to the floor."

"Mr. Pignati," John called again, knocking gently on the door now.

And what happened next almost gave me a thrombosis.

"Come in," an old man's voice demanded.

John and I grabbed each other as though we had just been sentenced to death. We watched in terror as the owner of the voice from the other side started to open the door.

Five

I don't know why Lorraine has to get so dramatic about
everything. I personally think it's all that dream interpretation she does. But whatever, the sound of that old
guy's voice made her turn stark white. The door slowly
opened and there they were—the same pair of dark
beady eyes Lorraine had claimed she had seen at the
window the day before. The eyes were set in a head
half hidden by shadows. And the head itself was set
upon a skinny and practically neckless frail body. The
hands that appeared in front of us looked rubbery, as
though they just rolled off at the end of his wrists. But
one thing was certain: this was no *ghost*. It was an
elderly bum who had obviously broken in and made
himself at home.

Lorraine and I and the hobo just stood there in a
staring match. Finally the bum spoke.

"If you don't mind, I'm going to sit down before I fall
down." This gruff voice emerged from the old lips.

Lorraine and I said nothing. I think we were more
embarrassed than anything else. Here we had expected
to see our dead Pigman, and we'd only made royal jerks
of ourselves. The old guy turned carefully and made his
way across the room to a dumpy chair by the bed. It
looked like a puff of wind could make him topple into
pieces like a snowman.

"I thought you were the guys from the Internal Revenue Service," he said, adjusting himself in the old
wicker chair. "Who are you kids?"

"We're sorry if we frightened you," I said, "but we
knew the man who used to own this house."

"*Frightened* me?" The bum sounded amused. "You
didn't frighten me. I was sleeping."

"But the bed isn't even rumpled," Lorraine observed
quickly.

"I don't have to answer to you. Or to your friend neither," the bum belched. "I don't happen to sleep in beds. I can't get up from a lying-down position. I like a chair. When you're my age, young lady, you'll know what I'm talking about."

"We're sorry, sir," I said.

"Yes, we are," Lorraine echoed. "We're very sorry."

There was a long pause, and I could see the disappointment in Lorraine's eyes as she surveyed the room. It was obvious this old guy had broken into the Pigman's house, and we weren't about to let him get away with it. I was just about to yell at him when the bum started yelling at *me*.

"All right, you nosy whippersnappers, you've had your look around. What do you want here?"

'I'm going to ask you the same question," I told him straight off. "What are *you* doing here? Why did *you* break in?"

"None of your business," the old guy yelled. "I saw you nosing around here yesterday. I may be old, but I'm not blind."

The bum was doing his best to really scream at us, but his lungs just didn't have it in them. He looked like he was crumpling right before our eyes. You could tell he was suffering. You could also tell he was angry.

"I'm waiting for an answer!" his voice finally said in a wheeze.

I decided to be a little respectful because of his age. I could see he was really no threat at all. "My name is John Conlan and this is Lorraine Jensen," I said proudly, deciding it was better to be truthful than tell him I was Prince Igor and that Lorraine was Lady Slobovia of Rumania.

"He's right," Lorraine piped in. "We were friends of Mr. Pignati, who used to live here."

"If he *used* to live here, which he doesn't now, then you must've come here to rob the place. Well, you're not going to rob *me*. You're trespassing just as much as I am!"

"We don't want to rob you," Lorraine said, sounding hurt that he'd even think such a thing.

"Ha, who are you kidding? Kids like you love to

crack old people over the heads with roller skates and rocks!"

"That's not true," I said. "We just came to look the place over; to remember all the good times we had with our friend. We didn't know somebody was *living* here."

"You mean 'squatting' here," Lorraine corrected.

"Well, now you do, so beat it!"

Lorraine and I looked at each other, and the old guy noticed the exchange of glances.

"You *are* from the Internal Revenue Service, aren't you?" He sounded terrified. "They're using kids now, aren't they? They send kids out to get the money. For God's sake, all I ask is to be left alone!" He rested his head against the top of the chair and closed his eyes. You could see that the old guy did have a neck after all. You could also tell he was on the run and hiding out.

"We're not from the IRS, sir," Lorraine stated. "We're just high-school kids, and we didn't come here to do any harm. We promise you we didn't."

"I think we'd better go," I told her, but I could see that Lorraine's sense of social work was now beginning to grow. I could just see this dossier growing in her mind.

Lorraine just kept staring at him. I thought her eyes were going to bulge out of their sockets and bounce across the floor. That's when I turned and looked at the guy again. He was just sitting there with his head back. His position looked extremely unnatural. More than that, he looked like he'd just kicked the bucket.

"Oh God," Lorraine said. "Do you think he's had a stroke?"

"Naw," I said.

"Oh my God, John, if he's dead, people are going to run around saying we killed *two* old men. They'll think we're the Zodiac Killer or somebody who drives around in a car knocking off old people. Take his pulse," Lorraine ordered.

I grabbed the old guy's wrist, trying as hard as I could to poke my finger into the right spot.

"John, you're not doing it right," Lorraine said, pushing me out of the way.

"Doing what right?" the old guy shouted, jumping to attention.

I dropped his hand as though it had just turned into a rattlesnake.

"We were only checking your pulse," Lorraine explained quickly.

"Checking my pulse?" the old man asked. "What—are you *nuts*?"

"We're sorry, sir," I offered as politely as I could.

"Well you should be," the old man said. "Barging in here when I'm resting. Trying to pick my pockets when I'm snoozing. I'll teach you!"

The old guy grabbed on to the arms of the chair and pushed himself up into a standing position. He reached over toward the bed and grabbed a wooden stick and started waving it at us. That's when Lorraine and I decided that retreat was the better part of valor. I mean, we didn't know what that old guy was really like then. And besides, he might have had a big sword tucked into the cane; or maybe he had a gun under the pillow. You never know what some of these old people will do. But what was even more likely was that if we let him chase after us, maybe he would really have gotten a stroke. And there was nothing in the world Lorraine and I would have wanted less than to have another guy croak on us.

Lorraine and I ran out of the room, practically leaped over the banister onto the stairs, and did double time all the way to the bottom floor. As we headed out the front door we heard the old guy's voice behind us, louder than he had managed to speak before.

"Don't you take anything down *there* either, you crooks!"

"Farewell, old house," I sadly mumbled as we ran out to the dilapidated porch and didn't stop before we hit the street. For some reason Lorraine was crying by that time. And we made a sharp right to leave the joint behind us.

"He'll never forgive us, John. Never."

"Who cares" I said. "He's a bum!"

"I don't mean *him*." Lorraine glared. "I mean the Pigman."

When she said that, I had an awful feeling come over me. I stopped and turned and looked back toward the house. Up at the window at the old guy standing there. His beady little eyes beaming down at us as if they were emitting death rays.

"It's the Pigman," Lorraine said. "That man is the Pigman *reincarnated*."

"He doesn't look like the Pigman. He looks like a *grouch*," I said.

"We're lucky he didn't come back as a hatchet murderer."

I took Lorraine's hand and we started off again fast down the street. Soon a cluster of tall evergreens hid the house so I didn't have to worry about those little antique eyes zeroing in on my back. We kept up a fast pace and only slowed when we passed Woodland Cemetery. Farther on down we simply walked at a normal pace, but without saying a word to each other. I knew Lorraine didn't really mean that the Pigman had been reincarnated, but who's to say? Nobody knows what happens after you die. Even that old evangelist I read about once who got buried with a telephone never made any calls. I often wonder who paid the phone bill, and how long they left it connected. Can you imagine having a phone put in your coffin? Do they give you a night light or what? And after they decide that you're really dead and aren't going to phone much, I wonder if any telephone man comes to pick up the equipment.

"I'm going home," I finally told Lorraine, breaking our strange, depressing silence. I usually don't ever admit that I have real emotion when I talk about myself, or write about things I do, but I must admit that there was some change going on inside of me. There was something bothering me. New feelings were beginning to take over, and I found it harder to tell a joke or be funny. I think maybe for the first time I was beginning to realize the story of John Conlan was the story of a boy who couldn't admit what he really felt inside, and told jokes instead.

"I'm going home," I repeated. I took one look at Lorraine and knew she understood that I had to be alone. We walked up the last part of the hill together, and Lorraine was biting her lip the whole way. I knew that it was a signal that she too had something on her mind, but I didn't feel as though I could bear hearing it. For some reason I just gave her a quick kiss on the cheek and said, "So long."

"See you," Lorraine said, heading for her house, looking as sad as I felt.

I went home and somehow made it through dinner without the Old Lady or Bore asking much more than if the downer expression on my face was because I'd failed a chemistry test or something. I told them I was depressed because I had seen a hit-and-run driver knock off a squirrel, but I don't think they believed me. Right after the eleven-o'clock news the phone rang, and I knew who it had to be.

"John, this is Lorraine." The voice came out of the receiver.

"What's up?"

"Well, I've been thinking about that old man," she started off. "I've come to the conclusion that his whole cranky attitude is just a defense mechanism."

"Who cares?" I said bluntly. Though somewhere deep inside me I knew that I really *did* care. I cared about the look of genuine fear on the old bum's face when he thought we were from the Internal Revenue Service. There was something very terrible that anyone that old would have to look that frightened in our society, although I didn't know why a bum would fear the IRS.

"In this magazine," Lorraine went on, "it says that elderly people sometimes only *look* cantankerous on the surface just so people won't like them. But they really *do* want people to like them. They're just afraid they're not going to be accepted, and being mean is a sign they're pleading for love."

"Maybe the geezer just doesn't like kids."

"You're just projecting," Lorraine corrected me. "You think nobody likes kids."

Somehow the truth of what was gnawing at me came slowly through. "Lorraine, you know as well as I do, that old man was planted there by Fate, just to punish us. He's a reminder of all the things we've done wrong. That's what he is."

24

"We didn't do anything wrong," Lorraine protested.

"I don't think that you or I believe that," I told her. "We never talk about it, but we should. Seeing that old bum in that house has made me feel sick to my stomach all night."

"That's just your guilt."

"Ha," I laughed. "Either that or the Old Lady's pork chops. And if you're not freaked out, then what are you calling me at this hour for?"

"John," Lorraine said solemnly. *"We have to go back there."*

"Oh *no* we don't."

"Please," Lorraine purred. "Please! I feel something is wrong. There must be some reason that old man picked out that house to hole up in. I don't know how to say it, but I think we're being given another chance. I think dead people work it that way. People die on you and then they send out vibes that give you another chance to make things better. I feel we're being given that chance."

Well, just let me say here and now that when Lorraine Jensen purrs at you and says "please" more than once, you know you've been purred at. I know from experience it's just easier to say, "Okay, Lorraine, whatever you say," even though I know at the end of whatever terrible thing happens, she'll end up blaming me for the whole thing.

The next day was Saturday. We had no school and were able to meet good and early at the corner of Eddy Street and Victory Boulevard. This time I wasn't so careful about what I was smoking, and Lorraine could tell right off it wasn't a spinach special.

"John, you promised to smoke the vegetable brand."

"I'm sorry," I said. "It's just too early to smoke spinach. If this was a good filter-tipped broccoli, maybe I could take it." Lorraine just gave me an infuriated look, and we started walking. The one thing I was not about to admit to her was that deep in my heart of hearts, I wanted to go back to that house as much as she did. I had thought about it all night. There was something strange about that old guy, the way he thought we'd been sent to check up on him. Maybe I had been

25

upset because I'd gotten too sentimental. He was probably nothing more than an old convict who had broken out of some jail someplace and mentioned the IRS to fake us out. He looked like one of the old aunts out of *Arsenic and Old Lace*. And I remembered those sweet old ladies used to run around giving arsenic to save people from the loneliness of life and then bury them in their cellar. But no matter what, I couldn't very well let Lorraine go over there by herself. It could be dangerous. He could be the most wanted senior citizen in the country. And who knew, maybe there was a reward. And if there was a reward, I knew Lorraine would want to split it with me.

"I think we should bring something with us," Lorraine instructed.

"How about a war-surplus can of knockout gas?" I suggested.

"John, I'm not kidding. I mean a present. Something to eat maybe." We ended up going to the nearest place, which was a dumpy drugstore that carried a line of Fanny Farmer candy at the intersection of Clove and Victory. The place was filled with the aroma of fudge near the candy counter. And a sour-looking saleslady came hot on our trail as though we were about to pick up a few things with five-finger discount.

"Can I help you?" she demanded more than asked.

"We'd like a pound of marble pecan fudge," Lorraine said. "And I hope it's fresh."

"Of course it is," the woman snapped, causing her hair to wiggle like an inverted mold of lemon Jell-O.

"Can we have a free sample of anything?" I inquired. "If it's good, maybe we'll buy that too."

"What are you, crazy?" the saleslady asked.

"Yes, I am," I told her. "Actually I'm the famous Grymes Hill Strangler just escaped from Bellevue."

The saleslady just snorted and didn't say another word. Not even "good-bye." I made a few grunts as I went out the door, and spun around a couple of times. That lady looked so mean she must have been raised on marble cake, brick ice cream, and rock candy.

By ten thirty we made it up to the house on Howard Avenue and knocked on the door. Nobody answered, but that didn't come as a surprise, knowing that the old guy might be in a stupor. Lorraine thought maybe he was sleeping, and I suggested we'd better look around first. We ended up going around the side of the house stepping over a herd of wild snails and checked out a few of the windows. Near the back of the house we found the kitchen window, and could see the old guy sitting at a table with a glass of acidophilus milk in front of him. He seemed completely absorbed in misery, and so thin I couldn't help patting Lorraine on the back and telling her that the fudge was just the thing to bring him. It was obvious that he had no real food.

Right then something furry ran over my feet, and I screamed, and when I screamed Lorraine screamed, and then we saw it was only a black cat. The old guy's head jerked around, and he started to get up. There was no time to think about an alternate plan of action, so we charged straight for the front porch. This time we scared the cat so much it shrieked as though it had just been sold to a Hong Kong Chinese restaurant. When we finally got our breathing under control, we advanced toward the front door and knocked. There was still no response.

"Perhaps he went for a cat nap," Lorraine whispered.

"Or to load a rifle," I suggested. I began to change my mind about the whole thing. "I think we should get out of here completely," I said, and I could see by the expression on Lorraine's face she was in no position to argue. I could hear her heart tap-dancing on the buttons on her sweater. As we turned to gracefully exit, a *creak* shot through the air. We whirled around and saw that the old guy had opened the front door. He had his beady little eyes fixed on us.

"I was waiting for you to come back," he growled.

Six

I looked at John, waiting for him to offer an explanation to the old man, but the expression on his face simply told me he was feeling sick again. He was probably having another rush of guilt about denying the fact that this old man was in trouble. He kept trying to say that the old guy was some kind of Jack the Ripper or something, but that was just avoiding the fact that he was an old man who needed us. *"Look beyond the words,"* I kept telling him. *"Look beyond his words."*

"I could have you both arrested for trespassing," the old man grumbled.

"We didn't mean to scare you," I said.

"No." John finally spoke up. "We were just checking out things because we thought something might be wrong when you didn't answer the door."

The old guy stood there staring. I noticed a brief twinkle in his eye. It was almost as if he was laughing at us, but that look faded.

"We brought you some fudge," I said, coming forward and offering the gift.

"What kind?" he snapped.

"Marble pecan, sir," John announced.

"Marble pecan?" the old man repeated slowly, almost taking each syllable apart. The twinkle in his eyes returned again. It was unmistakable this time. He started to smile and then stopped as if he were guarding himself with every word. "Well, I don't want your food. You young kids like to drug all us old people and then look through our shoe boxes for money."

"No, we don't," I said sincerely.

"Well, you can just get lost, because I'm a busted old man and I don't accept favors from strangers, especially kids. Wait till you're thirty before you come around to see me again," the old guy snarled. He started to close

28

the door. Neither John nor I did anything to stop him because we were so shocked by what the man had said. I felt terrible, because I knew that he must have been hurt a lot during his life. Once my mother and I lived near an old lady who smiled all the time and was nice to everyone, like I'm sure this old man must have been one day. Then this old lady's cat was poisoned one Christmas and she hardly ever came outside after that. Whenever I would play on my pogo stick outside her house, she'd open the window and shout that I was making too much noise. She used to make me cry because I'd never done anything wrong to her. The woman just never got over the murder of her cat, and I wanted to be able to say something to her but never could. And that's how I felt now. I think that's how John felt too, because he came closer to me and put his arm around my shoulder. Somehow when John touched me I felt again the kiss he had given me the night before—the kiss that reminded me of one of the most important things I've ever read in psychology, and that is that a person is what he does, not what he says.

"We were only trying to be *nice*," I was finally able to say to the old man.

"We want to help you," John added so gently I wanted to hug him.

"Why?" the man demanded to know, holding the door open just a crack now.

"Because you look like you don't have any friends." John just came out with it. "And you look like you haven't had a decent meal in two months!"

I felt an anxiety attack come on when John said that. He was so direct about it, almost angry, and *impatient* with the old man. But then I realized John was probably right in being so strong. The old man's eyes began to fill up with tears. I think he couldn't believe what John had said. There was a very long pause. It seemed like the computer of his brain was reaching back desperately to remember what it was like to trust another human being.

"You should be home with your parents," he finally said. "No use wasting time with an old man." He started to close the door again, and it must have been the way the light hit him, because we both noticed something blue and shiny swaying across his chest. John yelled, "Hey, what's that you're wearing around your neck?"

We could tell right away that we had hit a soft spot. The old man reached for the shiny thing. It was some sort of rock hanging on a beautiful gold chain. A flash of pride crossed his eyes as he slowly opened the door wider and wider.

"This?" he said. *"This was my life."*

John and I checked each other to see if either of us understood what he was talking about. We had no idea what the man meant. He didn't say anything after that. He just went back inside, but he left the door open. I looked at John again and I wasn't quite sure at first, but I remembered that actions speak louder than words. "He wants us to follow him," I whispered to John. In a flash John was dragging me along behind him into the house. We followed the old man into the living room. We weren't sure if he could hear us, because he seemed to behave as if no one was in the room. I think it was because he had to concentrate so much on each step he took. I was really afraid he might fall down.

When he did manage to sit it took him almost a full minute before he could adjust himself to a comfortable position. I just stood there holding the fudge out toward him. He stared at us again.

"Well, what are you doing here?" he asked. "And what are you standing for? We're not in Egypt. You're no mummies, and I'm certainly no pharaoh. Sit down over there before I strain my neck looking up at you all the time."

John went to the side of the room and sat on an old bench. It was very uncomfortable sitting totally across the room from the old guy and having him look at us as though we were mannequins in a department store. I began to have an anxiety attack again because I remembered an article I had read about an old man in Florida who invited teenagers into his house and ate them alive. Maybe this man was tricking us so he could make us into hors d'oeuvres or something. In any case, John must have picked up my internal panic, and he

30

took the fudge from my hand and placed it on a small table next to the old man. John sat back down on the bench and the old man looked directly at me.

"Come over here," he snapped, beckoning with his finger as though he was some kind of male witch.

"Me?" I asked.

"Yes, *you*," he said, fiddling now with the medallion around his neck. "I want you to help me take this thing off. My arms don't move so well." For a moment it seemed as though he smiled again. I saw he hadn't had much practice at smiling, because it seemed to strain his facial muscles in an unusual way. I looked at John and he flashed an *It's okay* message at me. I got up and moved slowly toward the old man. I watched his hands very carefully as I circled behind him and lifted the chain over his head. The sparkling mineral hanging on its gold thread almost hypnotized me.

"It's beautiful," I said, raising the dangling object high into the light, where its clusters of blue crystals sparkled brilliantly.

"Of course it's beautiful," he said; then he pointed to John. "*You*, move that bench closer. I'm not a ventriloquist. I can't shoot my voice to the moon, you know."

"Oh, sorry," John said, obeying his orders.

"*Look*, John," I said, swinging the shining rock toward him.

"What is it?" John asked.

"Primarily," the old man explained, "it's a fossil." The twinkle was beginning to grow in his eyes as he raised a finger to point out the details. "You see that raised sliver on the front? It's the horn tip of a prehistoric rhino. What you're holding in your hand is over twenty-five million years old."

"Wow," I said. John handed the fossil to me right away. I could see he didn't want to take any chances with it, and I didn't know what to do with it either. Just the way the old man talked about it I felt as though I was holding a piece of his heart in my hand, and that at any moment it would slip through my fingers and crash to the floor into a million pieces.

"No," the old man scolded, "don't be afraid of it. Run your finger over the rhino's horn."

31

He just stared at me and seemed to be waiting. I was afraid to do it because I thought at any moment I might be changed into a pumpkin or something. But finally I did as he told me, and it gave me chills knowing that my fingertips were actually touching something so old my mind couldn't even dream of it.

"You're touching one of the mysteries of the universe," the old man said joyfully. "Imagine being able to hold on to a part of life that was there long before you or I ever came into existence. It makes you think about where the force of life comes from." The old man's voice practically began to sing. "Certainly not from you or me. It's all out there, hiding, waiting to be known, perhaps only when we die."

It gave me chills to listen to him talk about death in Mr. Pignati's house. I even saw John shudder.

"Where did you get this?" I asked.

"Somebody gave it to me," the old man said slowly. "I used to dig a lot of fossils on my own too," he added. I felt now that his voice had grown guarded.

"You like digging?" John pursued.

"I always loved digging," the old man said. "At your age I couldn't get enough of it. I'd dig all over the place. I loved finding anything Mother Earth had hidden beneath her surface!"

I turned the fossil around in my hands, and I noticed a smooth polished area with printing on it set in the back of the blue crystals. I lifted the rock closer as though I was seeing things. Finally I was able to read it aloud: *To the Colonel, for fifty years of service*, the engraving said.

Suddenly the twinkle disappeared from the old man's eyes, and he reached out grabbing the gold chain. I leaped back as though I had been attacked, and now the old guy not only looked cranky, but he looked infuriated that I had noticed the engraving—as though he had forgotten about it. I scooted back next to John, who stood up fast. We both stood tense, ready to flee, but after a dreadfully long silence John squirmed and shot out as though nothing had happened at all, "You should come to our high school some time and help

Mrs. Stein teach a geology lesson." John sounded sincere in spite of what had happened. I breathed a sigh of awe and admiration for him, and I remembered why I had picked him for my friend to begin with. Whenever the going got rough, John Conlan was *there* to save the day.

"You need shock treatments," the old man growled, getting the chain back over his head until the fossil was again safely resting on his chest.

"You forgot about the fudge," John reminded the old guy, counting on helping the old man forget whatever had made him go as nuts as he did.

The old man laughed cruelly. "I didn't forget about it. You're just dying for me to open it so you can stuff yourselves with it. You just brought it for yourself, not me, buster."

I saw the look of sadness cross John's eyes, and I began to feel terrible for him. Every time John said something he had his head snapped off.

"Please, sir," I said with a voice that was barely audible, "have some of the fudge."

The old guy just stared at us. John and I looked at each other and now we were both very sad. We thought maybe we should just leave—that there really wasn't anything we could do. Just when we felt that we had totally failed, the old man reached out and ripped open the box of fudge. He started stuffing pieces into his mouth like there was no tomorrow.

John and I beamed. And John decided not to back away from the matter that had triggered the old man's anger to begin with.

"Who was the *Colonel*?" John asked loud and strong.

"What Colonel?" the old man sputtered while munching on the fudge.

"The fossil said *To the Colonel, for fifty years of service*," I reminded him.

The old man looked up and seemed ready to scream at me. The blood drained from his face again, and he looked like he was having an anxiety attack of his own. "The Colonel was a friend of mine," he said.

"The fossil belonged to *him*?" John asked.

The old man hesitated, shoved another piece of fudge into his mouth and spoke while chewing away. "Colonel Glenville and I were friends. We both like digging and I worked for him. He was a rich man once upon a time."

"How rich?" John wanted to know.

"You're a nosy little brat, aren't you?" the old guy said. "I'll tell you how rich Colonel Glenville was. He owned a town house in St. George, and he dug great tunnels under the earth. Colonel Glenville was a very famous man, and if you kids knew anything about history you'd know who he was. He designed eleven subway systems all over the world. He was knighted by the King of Sweden for the subway system he did in Stockholm."

"How exciting," I said. "But that must have been a long time ago."

"Why do you say that?" he demanded to know.

"I don't know," I said.

John jumped in to help me out: "Because everybody knows Sweden had subway systems a long time ago."

The old man didn't say anything. He just chewed away and suddenly his eyes looked far off, as though traveling back in time.

"What happened to the Colonel?" John asked as though he was onto something.

"Oh," the old guy said, "he died. I was with him a long time, and if you ever want to feel terrific you try living in a town house. Everybody wants to live in a town house. I tell you, I lived in a town house until . . . *a train ran over him!* That's what happened to him. I remember now, it was a train. That's one of the great ironies of life, don't you think? This man spends his whole life building subways, gets knighted by the King of Sweden. A terrific hole in the ground he built over there! And *bam!* Gets knocked off by a subway. That's life, isn't it?"

"Were you with him?" I asked.

"When he got run over by the train?" the old man asked as though I was crazy. "No, I wasn't with him! But I should have died the day of that crash, I'll tell you

34

that. When a man's work is ended—when no one wants to hire him anymore—his life is ended too."

Then a very remarkable thing happened. The old man opened his mouth as though he were about to call out for help, but instead he burst into tears. The tears ran down his face, and they led to great gasping sobs. I could barely understand the words that tried to escape through his profound sadness and mouthful of fudge. "*I want to go back. I want to go back,*" I thought I heard him cry.

"Have some more fudge," I heard John saying. I realized John's nerves were finally shot too.

"No," the old man sobbed.

"We really bought it for you," John said.

"No, thank you," the old man answered, readjusting his position in the chair. Slowly his sobs and tears died down, and he pulled a handkerchief from his pants pocket. We expected him to dab at his eyes or blow his nose, but instead he put the handkerchief over his face and held it there with his hands as though he was a person suffering a very great shame.

"I really think you should have another piece of fudge," John said softly. "Fudge has a lot of energy in it, you know. It's almost all sugar."

The old man shook his head negatively with the handkerchief still secured over his face. I could see John seemed not only disappointed, now, but frustrated because he hadn't been able to make friends with the old man yet. I've seen John meet a wild dog on the street and make friends with it faster than he was doing at the moment with the old man.

"Please, look at us," John almost begged.

"What for?" The voice came out from behind the handkerchief.

"We want to be your friends," John said as straight as an arrow.

The old man slowly lowered the handkerchief. John moved forward, lifting the box of fudge up toward the old man. The old guy reached down, took a piece, passed it under his nose as if he was savoring a fine cigar, and popped it into his mouth. He then looked at me and John and smiled. This time there seemed to be nothing forced about the glow on the man's face. He was truly smiling at us, *connecting* with us, and I could feel the electric message running through my veins that indeed our Pigman had come back.

I felt now as though I was going to interview a ghost. "Do you like to play games on the telephone?" I couldn't stop myself from asking. That was one thing our Pigman knew all about. The games we played, the riddles we liked, *jokes*; our Pigman knew all about jokes and riddles.

"What are you talking about?" the old man asked as though I was out of my mind.

"She means," John came to my support, "did you ever call a cigar store and ask if they have Muriel in a box, and when they say yes you tell them they'd better let her out before she suffocates."

John and I burst into laughter remembering how we used to do that before we met the Pigman.

"Or you call A&P store and ask them if they have peanut butter and *amatta*," I continued, "and when they ask, 'What's amatta?' you say 'I don't know. What's amatta with you?' "

John and I tried to laugh it up again, but the old guy still seemed to be a wet blanket in the humor department.

"Or the best one," John blurted, "you call some number from the phone book, and when they answer, you tell them you're the telephone repairman working on the line and that they shouldn't answer their phone for the next ten minutes or it will electrocute you—and then you hang up and call them right back and let it ring and ring until they do answer it—and then you let out a bloodcurdling scream, 'Ahhhhhh!' Did you ever do that?"

The old man looked completely puzzled. We had so many memories of the Pigman trying to keep up with the games we played, but this old man wasn't amused at all. We had no choice but to shut up and wait for him to say something so we'd know what was going on in his head. I was afraid that in some way we might have even scared him by telling him our corny jokes.

"The only game I know is the Game of Life," the old

man finally wheezed, and his words riveted us because that was really the kind of game that the Pigman would know about. He knew good games like how to remember things, and how to tell who was guilty in a crime; wonderful, intricate, mysterious games.

"How do you play that game?" John asked.

"You've got to get me a paper and pencil," he said.

John and I looked at each other and had a double attack of nostalgia, because paper-and-pencil games were specifically the Pigman's favorite. In fact I couldn't even move because an anxiety attack hit my feet. John raced around the room and dug up a piece of paper. I managed to activate my hands enough to find a half-chewed Papermate pen in my pocketbook. The old guy grabbed the paper and pen, and in a flash it seemed as though we were in a classroom. The old man was the teacher and John and I were just spellbound at his feet waiting, begging for the rules.

"You close your eyes," the old man said.

"Okay," John agreed, and his eyelids slammed down like a pair of well-greased venetian blinds.

"I can't close my eyes today," I said. "Maybe tomorrow."

"What do you mean you can't close your eyes?" the old man wanted to know.

"I'm too *nervous*," I admitted.

"Look, you've got to close your eyes to use your imagination," the old man ordered.

"I can't," I said.

"Then you're not going to play." He turned all his attention to John. "Now look, boy. The first thing you do is imagine yourself walking down a road. You've got to imagine the entire road, and really see yourself walking down it. Can you see it? Heh? *Can you?*"

"No," John said.

"Try, you dummy," the old man instructed.

"Oh, yeah," John finally said, his eyes still shut tight. "I see a road. I see a road and I'm walking down it."

"Okay," the old man continued, "what does the road look like?"

"It's thin, and it's winding. It's got cement curbs and there's a lot of jungle vines all over the place."

"Ha," the old man announced, and started doing some drawing on the piece of paper as though he was a psychologist. "That road is your Road of Life, and it means your life is a pretty hard one and it's not exactly clear. You don't know where the @#$% you're going, and there are wild animals lurking about. And the cement curbs mean you are a big mess of confusion and probably a lot of people are trying to cramp your style."

"Oh, yeah," John said, "that makes sense. It's probably my mother and father."

"Are they cruel?" the old guy wanted to know.

"Horrible," John said. "If I don't do everything they say, they rub Ben-Gay into my eyes!"

I felt like kicking John for being such a liar, but the old guy just moved right along anyway. "Keep your eyes shut," he ordered again, "and keep walking down the road until you see a key lying in the middle of it. Can you see a key?"

"Oh, yeah," John said. "I can see a key. I pick it up."

"What does it look like?"

"It's old, dirty, rusty, and bent."

"Now what do you do with it?"

"I throw it back down on the road and keep walking," John said.

"Well!" the old man exclaimed, as though John had just told him something he already suspected. "That key was the Key of Knowledge, and the way your key looks, it means you probably don't think too much of learning anything. You probably hate books and school. You're probably one of those smart-alecks who think they know it all when you're more likely nothing but a big dope."

"Or *maybe*," John countered, and I could see he was a bit angry at being called a dope, "*maybe* I don't like school because the *school* is old and rusty and a hundred years behind the times. Do you ever have anything like that in your Game of Life?"

"Look, I'm not going to argue with you, you know-it-all," the old man said, starting to put the paper and pen down as though he wanted to quit.

"No, look, let's go on," John said, changing his tone quickly, almost pleading.

"Please," I added.

The old guy grunted and sucked in a big breath of air. "All right. Keep your eyes shut and keep walking down the road now until you come to a cup. Do you see a cup?"

"Got it," John finally said.

"What does it look like?"

"It's Styrofoam, the kind you get at a hot-dog stand and bite pieces off so you can spit them out—and there's a soggy cigarette butt in the bottom."

"What do you do with it?"

"I try to clean it out because I'm thirsty, and I want to drink out of it."

"Good," the old man approved, nodding as though at last something was acceptable. "The cup, you see, is the Cup of Love, and your cup is in pretty rough shape, but at least you want to clean it up and start drinking out of it. But your cup is the cup of someone who probably sees love as pretty shaky, something that will fall into pieces and disappear. Somebody who thinks maybe his own love isn't worthwhile, but there's a flicker of hope in it for you because you're willing to try to clean it out."

I tried to keep my eyes from showing that I was more than routinely interested in the subject at hand. Also, you might as well know that this paragraph that I'm typing now is not going to be seen by John until after this whole memorial epic is finished, or he would probably tear it up—or be very embarrassed that I'm going to start telling you my true feelings about him. Up until now I never said very much about what I really feel for John except that he really is very good-looking, and I like it when he holds my hand because of the electricity and strength he gives me. And it's true, John and I have had a lot of adventures and have gone a lot of places together. We've been alone in cemeteries. We've been chased by the police from time to time. We've even discussed all the great issues of life, like death, love, careers, war, heaven, God, and school. We've gotten dressed up in adult clothes, and had candlelight dinner parties for just the two of us. We've had beer bashes for the neighborhood gang. We did a lot of silly

39

things and a lot of dangerous things. I just know it's not going to come as a surprise when I tell you that I've been in love with John for quite a while now. In fact some kids at school can't believe John and I haven't been making out like bandits with each other for years. And I'm not naive. I know that a lot of surveys and statistics on teenage sex would probably think we were both a couple of freaks if they knew that John and I had not been sleeping together, or even frolicking around in the backseats of cars. Maybe all the kids who will read this will say, "Boy, that Lorraine Jensen is a real waste," but I'm sorry, John Conlan and I have only been friends. Up to now all we've been is the two *best* friends in the world, and there are good reasons we never got more intimate than that. And anyone who says the way you were raised doesn't haunt you the rest of your life is nuts. There was one girl in school who used to act like a real loony tunes, and everybody hated her, but I knew there must have been a big problem in her past—and when I checked it out I found out that when she was eight years old her mother murdered her father. In my case you've got to understand that my mother hated my father for leaving her very shortly after I was born. And she spent a good deal of time teaching me that boys are dirty-minded and *sneaks*, and I'm not blaming her because if I had to live the life she did, trying to support myself and a kid without a husband, I would probably be a bit bitter and feel very cheated myself. And thank God she started to mellow out a bit this spring because of all the adult self-help books she's been reading, but she still hasn't gone to a psychologist. She still spends a great deal of time reinforcing in me the fear that all members of the male sex are out for one thing. Even though I know she's always been a bit crackers in the love department, it interferes with any romantic thoughts I have. Anytime I begin to have deep feelings for a boy, I can hear her voice in my mind saying things like "Don't let them touch you; boys are only out for one thing. Don't ever be left alone with a boy or he'll take advantage of you. Don't let a boy get you in his car or you'll end up pregnant. Don't kiss boys; you never know what germs they have on their lips. Sit with your knees together and ankles crossed or boys will think you're a slut." One thing I can tell you is if you go through your life hearing stuff like that, it can make you afraid of any man from Santa Claus to a priest. But if knowing our Pigman did anything for me, it at least taught me that kids are responsible for their own lives at a certain age. And that's exactly why I'm now able to admit to myself that I love John Conlan very, very much, and even though he doesn't know it, I'm going to do everything in my power to make him my own. I want to love him like I've always dreamed of loving a boy. I'm going to make John Conlan love me, even if it kills me. That's why I was particularly thrilled when the old man said there was still a flicker of hope for John when he didn't throw his Styrofoam Cup of Love away. (The end of my secret paragraph!)

"What do I do now?" John asked, his eyes still closed tightly.

The old man did a little more drawing on the piece of paper and spoke up. "You keep your eyes closed and walk farther down the road. Are you walking?"

"Yes."

"Good. Now you come to a tree on the side of the

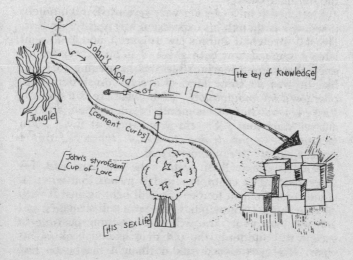

41

road. What kind of tree is it? What does it look like?"

John's face twisted as though he was straining to decide. "It's a big tree and there are shamrocks all over it. A lot of twisting roots and things, and a lot of leaves."

The old man smiled. "That tree is your sex life. It means your sex life will be rich and full. You'll be 'lucky in love,' as the expression goes."

I could feel my cheeks turn red and to my surprise I even saw John's face turn red, but that's a whole other story that I don't think he'll get around to telling you.

"Now keep walking down that road," the old man ordered, seeming especially curious at this time. His voice built as though he was about to reach the point in the game that he himself liked best of all. He was writing away a mile a minute. "You're walking down the road and you come to a wall. The wall is as thick as eternity and it's made of stone. It stretches as high as eternity. It runs below the ground as deep as eternity. And it stretches as far to the left as eternity, and as far to the right as eternity. Can you see this wall?"

"Got it," John admitted.

"What do you do with this wall blocking your road?" the old man asked.

I watched John's face get very serious. For a moment it seemed as though his expression was registering fear. His skin stretched and his jaw quivered, and a moment later it seemed taut with anger. I became very frightened that something horrible was happening to John, like he was on some kind of a crazy mushroom trip, *overdosed on imagination.* "John, what are you doing?" I asked. I watched as his mouth began to open, and the answer came out. "I'm throwing rocks at it. . . . I'm *kicking* it. . . . I'm *trying to smash the wall, but I can't! I can't!*" John almost cried!

"That is the wall of death," the old man said, his voice starting to crumple, "and it means that when it comes time for you to die, you will fight against it with all your might. You will fight and you will struggle, and you will claw at it. You will do everything possible to escape it!" Suddenly the old man leaned back in his chair. His eyes closed, and I thought maybe he had died. Instead he started to snore. The paper he had been drawing upon fell to the floor and I scooped it up. John and I looked at it and we could practically feel the Pigman had returned and was looking over our shoulders.

Seven

I resent Lorraine saying that my cheeks turned red when it turned out that I had seen such a terrific Tree of Sex. Maybe my face was red, but it wasn't because of the guy saying I was going to be lucky in love. It was because it was getting a little hot in the house. Besides, I was the only one wearing a sweater. The old guy was just sitting there in a pair of dark, shiny trousers and a shirt that looked like it had been borrowed from a bus driver. The poor old guy had some fudge and energy, and there wasn't much else we could do right then and there. But *no*, Lorraine was just itching to get us into trouble, to get us more involved. She stood there making a big fuss over the man like a vampire actress waiting for a character she could really sink her teeth into. Finally he came out of his stupor and I asked the guy his name.

"What?" the old man asked, like I was just inquiring about the most absurd thing in the world.

"I said, 'What's your *name?*' "

The old man looked like he was really straining his brain, and finally he whispered, "*Gus*."

"What?" Lorraine asked.

"*Gus*," he said again, this time more strongly. And suddenly he sat bolt upright in his chair, his eyes flickering with life. "I just had a vision," he said.

"A what?" I asked.

"A vision," he said. "Come closer. I can't keep straining my voice or it will disappear."

Lorraine and I did as he asked.

"What vision?" Lorraine wanted to know.

The old man closed his eyes for a second as though rechecking his images. When he spoke he sounded like a desperate little boy. "I need you to help me," he said. "I left something at the town house, and I need you to take me back there. My *trunk*. I need my *black trunk*."

I could see Lorraine's face light up. Even *my* nostrils twitched as though I sensed an adventure.

"How can we take you?" Lorraine asked. "Shall we call a cab? Or go to Eddy and Victory and take the bus?"

"I've got wheels," Gus said, sticking the rest of the fudge into his shirt pocket. He began to struggle with a dull-brown cardigan sweater, shoving his arms into the sleeves with excitement.

"Help me stand up," he ordered, "and get me to the garage."

Lorraine and I looked at each other, and this time we knew that unless we walked out of that house alone, just the two of us, and left the old guy there right that minute, we would end up getting so involved we could never let go until we knew his whole story. Lorraine made the decision for us as she moved quickly to one side of the old guy and I got on the other, and we became a pair of human crutches. We lifted him up onto his feet and then we started to walk him like a giant Barbie doll. Once we got him moving it seemed like his joints became greased and he was able to handle himself pretty well. We really only had to help him off the back porch to the yard. The garage doors looked like termite city, but when I flung them open there was a terrific beat-up canary-yellow old Studebaker convertible waiting inside.

"It's a honey, isn't it?" Gus asked.

"Oh, it's a honey," I said.

From the look of the car, I almost expected to see a sign on the rear bumper saying "See if you can hit me." And it was hard to tell which end was the front and which was the back.

"You can drive, can't you?" Gus wanted to know.

"Oh, *sure*," I said.

"John!" Lorraine screeched, her eyes giving me a look like I was insane. "John, I think you should tell the truth."

"I *am* telling the truth. Besides, this is no time to argue with your chauffeur. You know my father lets me drive the car." Of course Lorraine and I both knew that my father only lets me back his car out of the driveway on certain occasions like when there's too much snow and he doesn't want to get his feet wet. But I always felt that if I really got my hands on a car I would be a natural driver. A driver's license is only a piece of paper, I've been known to utter. And the point was that Gus needed us. Of course there were probably about 30,000 other old people hobbling around on Staten Island who could have used us too, but I figured we had a certain responsibility to the old guy since we did crash into the house and make the poor guy cry.

I got behind the wheel and put the old guy next to me, and Lorraine sat in the death seat on the far right. I was thrilled when Gus actually gave me the key. I put it in the ignition and turned it. I couldn't help looking past Gus to Lorraine as the engine began to turn over. She had fear written all over her face as the piston chambers commenced their little explosions ordinarily known as starting. The clanking and coughing were earsplitting.

"Purrs like a kitten," Gus sighed.

"Be careful, John," Lorraine kept saying over and over again. "Be careful, be careful . . ."

Well I tell you, we had no trouble getting out of the driveway. I only stalled seven times, and before you knew it we were rolling down the hill towards Louis Street. Part of the way we were *literally* rolling because the engine had quit, but I finally managed to start the car and get the pistons crashing away again. Within five minutes I was driving like a pro and hardly ever swerved over the center line. I think any cop on Staten Island could have seen me drive by and thought I was at least twenty-five years old, with many years of driving experience behind me, and one thing I found out from pumping the accelerator straight off was that I would never get arrested for speeding. On a straightaway I tried to floor it, but it took a block before I hit twenty miles an hour.

"Lorraine, you can tell your facial capillaries to let the blood back into them," I told her.

"Please be careful" was all she kept repeating.

"Do you mind if we put the top down?" I asked Gus.

"Love it," he said.

"I don't think we should," Lorraine advised.

I immediately pulled over and unsnapped the roof. I even knew enough to gas the engine while I pulled the little button, and *wango!* the roof leaped up into the air like a dragon opening its mouth. I could have sat there all day just watching that roof go up and down, seeing the plastic rear window fold into place. The motor that drove the roof made twice as much noise as the car engine, and I saw at least three people walking on the street stop and stare. To me it was like a fantasy coming true. I had always had a dream that I would be behind the wheel of a convertible driving up and down Victory Boulevard, and all the kids from school would be made to stand along the curb and applaud me as I drove up and down. In my dream I am usually in a Mercedes-Benz or Rolls-Royce, but I figure a kid's got to start someplace.

I pulled back out into a lane of traffic. By the time I finished that maneuver I looked over and I thought Gus had dropped dead; instead he was sleeping. I thought it was terrific the way the old guy could catch a snooze whenever he felt like it. A couple of raindrops started to fall, but if anyone thought I was going to put the top back up on the car they were crazy. Besides, I saw there weren't enough clouds in the sky for it to really pour, but the wind sure picked up and the car started to swing in the breeze. Near the bottom of Victory Boulevard I had to make a sharp turn to the right. That's when Gus fell over and his head dropped right into Lorraine's lap. She let out a scream as though someone had just dropped a bucket of worms on her, and looked absolutely absurd trying to push him back up into a sitting position.

"Are you sure he isn't dead?" Lorraine gasped.

"No, he's snoring. Just listen hard."

"John, where are we going?"

"Look, the town house is in St. George, right? He just wants to get some black trunk. Check the glove compartment."

Lorraine pounded the glove compartment until it finally plopped open. She went through a pack of manuals and pamphlets until she found a registration. We were surprised to see it wasn't in Gus's name, but it would do. She read aloud. "Glenville, Parker, 107 Stuyvesant Place."

"Oh, yeah, that's got to be right down by the museum. Do you remember in biology when Miss Bensen took the whole class down there to see all those stuffed birds of America?" I reminded her.

"John, it's *raining*," Lorraine insisted on pointing out.

"It will be over in a minute."

"Put the top up."

"Then nobody can see us."

"John, you're crazy."

I took a quick glance in the backseat because subliminally I had noticed a lot of junk on the floor. There were some tools, loose papers, and ripped shopping bags. I also saw the handle of an umbrella.

"Use the umbrella," I ordered, "the umbrella on the backseat."

Lorraine looked at me as though I had just told her to eat a cockroach. "I'm not going to use an umbrella in a convertible just because you don't want to put the top up."

"Then get wet," I suggested.

"John, this is insane," she babbled as she turned and reached over to grab the umbrella. "You are going to get the old man wet and he'll die of pneumonia."

"It's going to stop any minute."

"John, I feel ridiculous," she said emphatically, as she pressed the little button near the umbrella handle and it opened up its huge black ribbed form.

"Look at the people look *now*," I pointed out.

"Oh, they're looking all right," Lorraine bellowed over the engine. I had to swerve again quickly to the left and Gus' head fell forward again and crashed into Lorraine's lap. She was quite a sight trying to right him with one hand. And then I had to make a right, so his head came flying over and crashed onto my shoulder.

"John, if you don't turn more carefully, you're going to break his neck."

Suddenly a black cat came running out into the road

in front of us and I smashed on the brakes. I stopped just in time and the cat moved slightly to the right of the front fender and stared at us as though it needed a quick visit to an exorcist.

"John, I just know this is an omen," Lorraine said.

"Lorraine, please keep your omens to yourself while I'm driving. This road isn't exactly a picnic."

"Ah, my old town," Gus said suddenly, his head lifting up off my shoulder. "Can you smell that fresh sea air?" Lorraine and I looked at the speaking old head between us. By this time we were heading down Hyatt Street and could see the Statue of Liberty and New York Bay. Also right in front of us was Borough Hall, and beyond that the Staten Island Ferry Terminal. There were also a couple of wild bars right there where all the Coast Guard guys and shipyard workers get drunk and beat each other up so you read about it the next day in the *Staten Island Advance*.

"Turn down *there*," Gus ordered.

"You got it," I said. I tugged at the wheel and made a sharp tangent from the left lane to the right, causing a chorus of burnt rubber to be chanted by a couple of cars that were close behind me.

"That's my boy!" Gus said a couple times, slapping my knee. "That's my boy! This calls for a piece of fudge!" He reached into his shirt pocket and passed each of us a piece. He pushed three pieces into his mouth and began to chew like a trouper. Gus was beginning to get so excited it seemed the old-man part of him was just leaping out of his body, leaving behind a youngster. He was really beginning to remind us of the Pigman now. He was singing away, "La, la, la, la, la." Before you knew it the old guy had Lorraine and me joining in with him. The old Studebaker kept coughing out its *chug-a-lug-lug*, and we tried to keep our singing to the beat of the pistons. "La, la, la, la, la." He didn't even complain that it was raining and all we had was an umbrella up. I suppose it was right about that second that I decided this old guy was really turning out to be all right.

"Okay, quick!" the old guy ordered, "shoot this corner like a whip."

I figured that meant turn again. Now we were on Stuyvesant Place. The Studebaker seemed to bend around the corner at the same angle as our bodies rather than lift itself on two wheels like an ordinary car would. Now the street turned into the only section on Staten Island that really looked sophisticated. A bunch of town houses all in a row, most of them looking like they could use some good sandblasting. They were packed next to each other like sardines in a can, and a lot of them had wrought-iron bars on the lower floors because there are a lot of crooks who run around the St. George area. The favorite sport of the kids on Staten Island is breaking and entering, and their second-favorite sport is beating up kids from New Jersey.

The rain had stopped and the street was covered with a smoking mist rising from the asphalt. It made me feel I was driving through an old movie. I was the romantic detective with a cigarette butt hanging from my lip, and Lorraine was my nosy girl Friday who was along for the ride. If only we had helped the Pigman this way, maybe the terrible things that happened to him wouldn't have happened.

"*Brakes!*" the old guy yelled. "Brakes!"

I slid to a perfect stop in front of 107 Stuyvesant Place. There was the town house, five stories of dark stone that looked like a private sanatorium for indigent berserk persons.

"Oh, my God, look what they did to her," Gus said sadly.

There were boards and "Condemned" signs covering everything, and it took a while to get used to the sight. To tell the truth I was expecting the old guy to break down crying. But the three of us got out and he just leaned against the car shaking a mean fist at the house. Lorraine and I didn't know what to say. We thought it was best to let Gus have his little reverie, and then we could be on our way again.

"Come on," he said, "we're going *in*."

He reached out his hands to us, and once again we became his crutches. We walked down the steps that led to the basement. It was one of those jobs where, beneath a set of stairs going up to the main floor, there are steps that lead down to the basement. There was an iron gate protecting that area, and Gus shoved a key in my hand. "Open it," he ordered.

I hesitated because I didn't want to let go of him.

"Don't worry about me," he blurted. "I can handle myself from here on in. Get that gate open and throw a garbage can through the window."

"*Gus*," Lorraine said, "don't you have a key for the door?"

"I lost it," Gus yelled, "but my whole life is in this house, and nobody's going to take it away from me without a fight!"

I took the key and opened the gate. A shot of energy ran through the old man and he broke away from Lorraine. Before we could stop him he actually lifted a garbage can and hurled it at the window. The can bounced off the middle frame but shattered two huge panes of glass. The glass and the garbage can crashed onto the cement patio like an explosion.

"Somebody will call the police," Lorraine cried out.

"Ha," Gus said. "My neighbors wouldn't call the police if maniacs were setting me on fire!"

A car honked on the street several times then. The three of us froze. We heard steps on the pavement. I peeked around from under the steps and all I could see was a woman across the street getting into some car. Somebody was double-parked and a few cars had come to a stop behind them. They started honking, and after some loud verbal exchanges they all drove off.

"Climb in and unlock the basement door," Gus ordered.

"We'll be shot for trespassing," Lorraine moaned.

"Did they really lock your trunk up inside?" I asked Gus.

"Yes," he said. I could tell by the look in his eyes that he wasn't lying.

"Then you're going to get it back," I said, and I knocked away the glass and climbed in.

The front room of the basement was dark with stabs of light flying through from the boarded windows. I took one breath of the dark, cold air and hurried to the door. I fumbled with the locks, waiting for a rat to run over my feet, but managed to get it open before anything bit me.

"Now we're in business," Gus cheered as he rushed in. Lorraine stepped gingerly behind him.

"Did they board the place up right after the Colonel died?" I asked, but the old guy ignored me and kept saying, "We'll show them. We'll show them." He went straight to a workbench in the far left corner of the basement.

"This feels like a *real* haunted house," Lorraine said. But then I could see she regretted it, because Gus obviously loved the house. She mumbled an apology immediately, but Gus paid no attention to us for the next few moments while he was testing flashlights with various degrees of battery strength. I moved in to get a closer look at what was the best collection of flashlights and lanterns I'd ever seen. He must have had seventeen regular flashlights and two or three bigger contraptions. I started testing them along with him, and when I found a couple that were pretty good I gave one to Lorraine. The old guy took a big lantern for himself.

"I built this area of the house myself," Gus said, pointing to built-in filing cabinets. He pulled out this long drawer that resembled a refrigerated compartment in a morgue. "These are the designs for some of the subways I did," he babbled. His voice sounded stronger as he grasped a cluster of long vinyl tubes and slipped out some blueprints. There were so many arcs and lines and angles and notations it gave me a headache to look at them with only the illumination of a couple of flashlights.

"How long does it take to draw something like that?" I asked.

"Almost a year," Gus answered solemnly.

"That long?" Lorraine asked incredulously.

"The Colonel wasn't a hack," Gus bellowed.

"I'm sure he wasn't," Lorraine agreed.

Gus dumped the whole mess of plans back in the drawer and slammed it shut. He turned his lantern and followed the light beam, with us straight behind him. We proceeded down a dark narrow hallway, made a sharp right turn, then a sharp left, and found ourselves in a rectangular-shaped room with cushiony sofas and lots of pillows on them. Then a little farther down another hall was a kitchenette off to the right, but we didn't go in there. Instead we kept going straight until we reached these dusty old drapes. Gus pulled a string and the drapes parted, to reveal sliding glass doors and a rear patio beyond.

"That was the garden," Gus pointed out.

Lorraine and I pressed our faces to the window. The garden outside was very eerie-looking, or maybe it was just the darkness of the rain clouds hovering above. There were these long vines hanging all over the place that looked like mutated octopuses. They covered the white wrought-iron furniture that wasn't so white anymore. And on both sides of the garden there were these strange statues. One had the body of a horse and the head of a man, and the other one was this voluptuous woman who the old guy said was Venus. I was expecting a whole bunch of violinists to show up and start playing the first act of *The Nutcracker*. Gus was really getting very freaky, I thought. He not only did not need us as crutches, he could have used roller skates at the rate he was traveling. He led us back down the hallway into the kitchenette. Beyond that was a dark archway where I could glimpse some stairs heading up into the house. We went through the arch and Lorraine let out a big scream. I mean what greeted us on the other side wasn't what you'd ordinarily expect to find at the foot of a staircase. And I was surprised to hear Gus chuckle. We had come face to face with a giant plaque on the wall that was a full-color, three-dimensional, four-foot dinosaur. It had a little gold plate underneath it that said it was a STEGOSAURUS. But it looked like a plain old spiky lizard to me. "The Philadephia museum gave that to the Colonel," Gus said, "because he was putting in a subway down there and found the hipbone to that thing."

Gus started up the stairs. Lorraine and I hurried to his side just in case he decided to go to sleep and fall backward. It was a weird sensation walking up partially carpeted marble, and when we got to the top Lorraine and I had to rest against the banister. Lorraine let out another shriek. This time there was a PLESIOSAURUS on the wall.

Gus laughed. "The Colonel really loved the dinosaurs. *He really loved them.*" Then he took off and we had to practically trot to keep up with him. He went into a large room at the front of the house. We all spun our flashlights in different directions, and I couldn't believe my eyes. The walls were made of crocodile skin. There was even a guest book made with a crocodile-skin cover, stationed on a podium near the front of the room. It looked like the Colonel must have really been loaded, and maybe a little nuts too.

"This room was imported from Tanganyika," Gus bragged. "It was the Colonel's favorite room."

Bam! Gus was off again. We rushed after him this was and that way. Sometimes running into closets or dead ends in bathrooms. It felt like we were journeying through tunnels. On the next floor Gus pointed out the Colonel's office in the back of the house, red- and blue- and green-colored glass covering the entire back wall. The slivers of glass sparkled like rubies and amethysts and emeralds; either that or a lot of cut-up old soda bottles. The room was flooded with intricately designed woodwork—the kind my mother would have adored spraying Johnson's wax on.

"This room was imported from England," Gus stated. "You can't get mahogany like this anymore."

"Gus," Lorraine said soberly, "I think we'd better get your trunk and get out of here. Someone may have heard us breaking in."

"Well, I'm tired," Gus complained, plopping down into a big swivel chair behind the desk.

"We'll get it for you," I said. "Where is it?"

"Just keep going up the stairs to the top floor," Gus said. "You can't miss it. The *black* one."

"What if there's an alarm system or something Gus doesn't know about?" Lorraine whined.

"Don't worry about it," I said, grabbing her hand and dragging her to the stairs. I held on to her and had to practically yank her all the way up the next flight. There was a little hall and it seemed like this floor had been divided only into two rooms. The rear room was huge. I flashed my light around and saw that it was a bedroom. A huge four-poster bed was sitting smack in the middle of the floor. A semicircular window was set in one wall, and it was made up of at least forty little framed windows. There was an old-fashioned telescope planted right at the foot of the window. Lorraine and I went over to try the thing out immediately, but there wasn't a crack wide enough in the shutters, which had been nailed shut from outside.

"This room is creepy," Lorraine said.

"Why do you say that?" I asked.

"I don't know," she said. "I think it's because I get the feeling no woman ever lived here. I get the feeling there was never a woman in any part of the house."

"Did some ghost tell you?" I asked.

"No," she said. "The house is too rugged. There's nothing feminine. Nothing soft and delicate. There's something frightening about it. I just don't think a woman would put up with all the wood and dinosaurs."

"If you plan on having an anxiety attack," I told her, "I wish you'd save it awhile."

Lorraine let go of my hand and walked closer to the bed. She touched one of the huge posts, which practically stabbed its way through the ceiling. "I feel like I'm standing in a mausoleum," Lorraine said. "That's what this is."

"Come on."

"I mean it, John. This place is some kind of shrine to all the Colonel's achievements. There's nothing really *lovely* here." She moved the flashlight to a corner of the room. A glass cabinet sparkled and we hurried to it. It was a store display case with several medals of honor lying on black-velvet backgrounds. It looked like a ten-year supply of graduation honors, tons of awards from all over the world honoring Colonel Parker Glenville. I opened a huge wooden thing that must have been a closet of some sort because it was filled with old uniforms.

"The Colonel must have been a tall, thin man," Lorraine said, her eyes sizing up the clothes. "Look at the jackets. They could fit you."

I grunted and took her hand to get her out of there. We moved back into the hall and were just about to enter the front section when Lorraine let out another scream. This time it was a full-blown model of the IGUANODON, according to the plaque hanging right beneath its open mouth. It looked like a cross between a turtle and a lizard. Its glassy stare was the kind of thing nightmares are made of.

We moved forward into the front room. It was filled with a lot of packed boxes and several trunks of varying shapes and sizes. I kicked a few of the trunks lightly with my foot, but they each gave back a hollow ring. Then Lorraine flashed her light onto a black one with leatherette covering. I gave it a kick, and there was no doubt that this one was packed full. I stooped down and started to flip open the locks. Lifting the top, I was sure it was the trunk Gus wanted. I started rummaging through it.

"John, what are you doing?"

"Just checking."

"John, we have no right."

Right on the top was a long yellow tassel, the type an officer would wear on his shoulder. It looked like Gus wanted to take a memento of the Colonel with him, which was nice, I figured. There was a big pile of clothes underneath that looked like they could use a few years in a General Electric washing machine. Then there was a box of weird-looking tools—points and curves and angles. I figured they must have been some of the tools of the Colonel's trade, and I supposed there was no harm in Gus sucking them up too. After all, the Colonel was no longer going to use them, and it was probably better that an old friend got them. Next to them was a ratty wooden cigar box that contained a bunch of old silver dollars. They all had dates like 1883 and 1867 on them. I think that about this point I had to admit that Gus was getting into the area of what could be called theft.

"John, you can't let Gus take some of those things. Those are the kinds of things that belong in the Colonel's estate, and I'm sure courts and lawyers and all kinds of people like that would put us in reform school if we helped Gus steal them!"

Just then a cold weird wind began to blow in the

56

room. There were no windows open. But we could feel this chilling breeze, and the dust moved around us enough to give us a minor choking fit.

"John, I feel as if there is someone else in the room with us now," Lorraine whispered, turning rapidly and flashing her light all about.

I felt the hair begin to bristle on the back of my neck, and I was about to close the trunk when I noticed a white envelope strapped against the lid. I lifted it up, opened it, and took out one of those folders that look like they're going to hold a highschool prom picture. Lorraine practically ripped it out of my hand, and opened it to reveal a very old picture of a man with a beard. The man was in a uniform and he was saluting. There was a big grin on his face. A grin that was at least thirty or forty years younger than the one on the man we knew, who was sitting downstairs in a swivel chair. Engraved in gold letters beneath the photograph was "Colonel Parker Glenville," and we knew then that indeed the Colonel was not dead. *Our Gus was the Colonel.*

Eight

I couldn't stop John from rummaging through that trunk for another five minutes. He's one of the nosiest boys I've ever seen, and I was on the verge of having a huge anxiety attack. I had to go to the front window and breathe a few extra millimeters of fresh air that leaked in around the sills. The louvers on one of the outside screens were turned in a way so I could glimpse the street below. I was expecting to see a police car, but instead there was nothing but a scrawny German shepherd moping down the sidewalk. I bent my head to see if anybody was across the street, and managed to glimpse the figure of a real bum. This destitute old man seemed to have nothing to his name but a pile of blankets that he was clutching, and he was drinking a bottle of wine as he went along his way. He looked so solemn and awful, I couldn't help wondering if he was one of those ordinary bums or one of those extremely intelligent people who had become so disillusioned by society that he just couldn't handle his life anymore.

When John was good and ready, he engineered our exit. I never felt more mortified than when he made me help him drag the trunk down the outside steps while people were walking back and forth on the street. I don't know what *he* thought they could think, but *I* knew what they thought—seeing a couple of kids yanking this big leatherette trunk out of a boarded-up, dilapidated town house. When we finally got the thing all the way to the rear of the Studebaker we couldn't even open the car trunk'

"Kick it," Gus yelled, as he came down the steps to the sidewalk, still under his own power.

We tried a few times until John kicked just the right spot and the car trunk flew open. We swung the trunk inside, closed everything up, and John ran around to open the car door for me. I went to slide in but stopped short. The German shepherd I had seen from the upstairs window was now lying on the backseat of the old convertible. He was literally sprawled across the cushions, his head buried in his front paws. He had obviously jumped in and made himself entirely at home. He had two of the saddest eyes in the world and looked like he was suffering' from a persecution complex. I should have known there was a reason he had picked this particular car.

"*Get out*," John yelled at the dog. The dog wouldn't budge. By now the old man was at our side, and I figured when he saw the dog he'd probably pick up a stick and smack him for trespassing. Instead Gus' eyes began to twinkle. And the dog's eyes brightened too. Gus immediately grabbed a piece of fudge out of his pocket and offered it to the dog, saying, "You're a good boy. You're a good boy." The dog accepted the offering and began chewing it as though he was a connoisseur of sweets.

"Come on now, *get out*," John ordered the dog.

"He's okay," Gus said.

"What do you mean, he's okay?" John wanted to know. "Get out! Get out!" he yelled at the dog again.

"John, let's get out of here. We can dump the dog later," I suggested. "The police are coming. You can let the dog out down the block."

"*Let the dog come with us*," Gus demanded.

I was really getting worried now, because I could see the headline, "Lorraine Jensen Mutilated by Mad Dog." But I got in. John took the old man around to his side, shoved him in next to me, then got behind the wheel again. He started the engine, and we took off with the old man yelling happily, "We'll fix the IRS! We'll fix the IRS!" The very next thing he did was fall asleep. I couldn't believe how Gus could be jumping around one minute, and snoring to beat the band the next. John turned the car sharply right and then he turned it left, and the Colonel's head began to roll between us once more like it was in a Ping-Pong tournament. Then the Colonel's head crashed against my shoulder and stayed there for five minutes as we began to climb up Victory

Boulevard and out of St. George. I was thankful when we had to make a sharp right and Gus' head went flying onto John's shoulder. I couldn't help watching the two of them while I massaged the circulation back into my clavicle. They made quite a picture. Even with their ages so far apart there was something very similar about the two of them. Something of destiny, perhaps. It was that their noses were alike even though Gus' nose was older than John's. Maybe it was the strong look of determination in their faces. But whatever, the position of Gus' head on John's shoulder made Gus look like a little boy resting against his father.

It started to drizzle again and I opened up the umbrella. The dog began to whimper as though he was afraid of rain. I turned around to pet him, to reassure him that everything was all right. I was also concerned that he not get carsick. He started to lick my hand, and I rubbed his forehead. Then the dog barked, and I could just tell he wanted another piece of fudge. I reached into Gus's pocket and found the last little squashed piece. I gave it to him, and as he chewed it the expression in his eyes was that of a pooch in canine heaven.

I was really thankful that John got us back to Howard Avenue and the garage in one piece. He shut off the motor, and Gus was still sleeping. John thought it was better to just leave him in the car for a few minutes while we pulled the trunk inside and upstairs. When we came back out we found the dog stationed at the open door of the car as though he was a guard. I petted him a few times to show how grateful I was for protecting the old guy, and John started tapping Gus on the shoulder to wake him up.

"Gus," he called over and over. "Come on, Gus, you're home."

Gus didn't budge, but every single time John called "Gus," the dog barked and looked at us as if he expected another piece of fudge to be offered.

"John, I think his name is Gus."

The dog barked.

"Who?"

"The dog."

"Gus?" John asked.

The dog barked again.

"The *dog* is Gus," I repeated. "I think the *dog* is the real Gus! He must have been the Colonel's dog and gotten lost when the Colonel had to clear out of the town house."

"Gus?" John called.

The dog just wagged his tail and barked as though he was home again at last.

Nine

At first I thought Lorraine was bananas, but sure enough, every time I said "Gus" the dog would bark, and perk up, and look at me and wag his tail. At one point he ran right to my side with his tongue hanging out of his mouth. I realized of course this *had* to be the Colonel's dog, which is why the poor mutt was sitting in the back of the car waiting for us.

"Do you know how to wake up the Colonel?" I asked.

Gus barked, then jumped past me back into the car and started licking the Colonel's face. It took no more than a few seconds to revive the old man, and he woke up patting the dog on the head. "That's my boy," the old man kept saying over and over again, "that's my boy." Then the Colonel ordered us to help him out of the car. All the energy he'd seemed to have at the town house was gone. Lorraine and I lined up like crutches again and were as gentle as we could be. We got him inside the house and up the stairs, and all the while he kept telling us how nice it was going to be to have a dog around the house. When he reached his bedroom, he seemed almost surprised to find his trunk waiting for him. I tucked him into his chair and Lorraine took a blanket and covered his legs. Then I pulled down the shades to darken the room. Lorraine and I were just about ready to give him some peace and quiet when I heard him call us back. We moved close to him.

"What is it?" I asked.

There was a long pause.

"Good night, John," he whispered. "Good night, Lorraine."

"Good night, *Colonel*," we said softly, even though it wasn't nighttime at all.

He looked at us as if he couldn't be sure he had heard us call him the Colonel. We hadn't meant to; it just happened. He turned away for a moment, and his eyes filled up with tears. Then he looked directly back at us. We reached out and took his hand and stayed with him until he fell asleep.

I told Lorraine to watch him while I took a quick run down to the little A&P. She didn't really like the idea of being left alone in the house, but when I told her what we had on our hands was not a ghost, but a very real old man who had probably gone broke because he couldn't pay taxes on the town house or come up with taxes on his income to the IRS, I think she found those earthly reasons enough. Besides, she had Gus, the German shepherd, and he looked like he'd fight to the death to protect the Colonel and Lorraine as well. I had only four dollars and thirty-seven cents, so I bought grapefruit juice, a half dozen eggs, a quarter pound of butter, a half gallon of acidophilus milk, two cans of Campbell's tomato soup, one loaf of bread, and two dozen chocolate donuts, which had been marked down because they were a little crushed. As I carried the stuff back up Howard Avenue, I wished I had taken the Studebaker, but somehow it didn't seem right unless the old man was with me. It not only didn't seem right, it seemed much more dangerous because I think cops pull a young kid driving alone over faster than they do if they see a kid with an old person. When I got back to the house Lorraine was already scrubbing out the refrigerator to make room for the fresh food. She looked really happy that I had bought eggs, and decided to boil all six of them. "We can all have dinner together," she said, "and bring the Colonel over some more food tomorrow. My mother's got a lot of canned goods stored up." While the eggs were cooling, I mopped the kitchen floor while Lorraine tried dusting the living room. It all looked like a losing battle, but at least it would be a little fresher and cleaner for the old man. I was just wiping down the windowsills when we heard the Colonel scream out in pain.

"Oh, my God." Lorraine forze.

I pushed past her and ran up the stairs two steps at a time. "What is it? What is it?" Lorraine called, now breaking into motion fast behind me. The thumping of my feet on the stairs didn't drown out another scream from the Colonel. And another!

I burst into the Colonel's room. He was bent over in his chair clutching his stomach, moaning deeply, loudly.

"What's the matter?" I cried out.

The Colonel strained to lift his face to me. It was shattered with pain. I didn't know what to do. Lorraine was at my side saying, "What's the matter? What's wrong?" The Colonel couldn't speak, and I didn't know if I should just run across the street and bang on the door of the convent; or maybe I should just tell Lorraine to run into the middle of the street and stop traffic and say, "Help! Help!" Finally words began to emerge from the Colonel. He said something about cramps in his stomach. And then I heard very clearly "Get me to a hospital."

"Grab him," I ordered Lorraine. She hesitated. I could see she was frightened. "*Grab him!*" I ordered again, and in a flash we became the old man's crutches once more.

He cried out louder as we lifted him from the chair.

"We've got to get him into the car," I said.

"Hurry," the Colonel moaned, "hurry!"

Somehow we managed to get him down the stairs. We practically lifted him into the air. We knew it wasn't just indigestion, or something simple like that. We knew it had to be a matter of life and death. Gus was waiting for us at the bottom of the stairs, barking. He jumped up on my shoulders and kept kissing the back of the Colonel's neck as we got him to the side door. That dog had the longest tongue I've ever seen in my life, and I never saw a dog love anyone the way he loved this old guy. I had to move fast to close the door so the dog wouldn't follow us out into the car. In another minute we were in the Studebaker, and I had the key in the ignition. The pistons began to explode again, and as we pulled out of the driveway, I could hear Gus barking frantically now from within the house. Lorraine had taken some Kleenexes out of her pocketbook and was helping dab the old man's forehead.

"It's going to be all right," she kept saying. "It's going to be all right." The old man just kept moaning.

"I need an emergency room," he wheezed, "an emergency room."

"It's all our fault," Lorraine said.

"You're crazy," I snapped.

"It's the fudge. You're not supposed to give fudge to anybody who drinks acidophilus milk," Lorraine moaned.

"I don't even know what acidophilus milk is," I countered.

The Colonel let out a piercing shriek of pain just as we turned the corner onto Clove Road. A group of Boy Scouts was standing on the corner just shooting the breeze until they heard the scream. Then they all looked up, amazed, as though they had just flunked Advanced Knotting. In another couple of minutes I had the old Studebaker crashing up the emergency ramp to Richmond Hospital. A couple of attendants were right by the entrance sneaking a smoke, but I jammed on the brakes and they came galloping to help us.

"Don't tell them I'm the Colonel," the old man said through his pain. "Don't give them my real name."

In two shakes of a lamb's tail the attendants had the old guy on a stretcher with wheels and flew him through these automatic doors. Lorraine and I trotted behind, but to our surprise the procession came to a rapid stop in front of an admissions desk.

"What seems to be the problem?" this mean-looking nurse asked us. The Colonel couldn't talk, and you could see he was trying to hold back his anguish, but he still had to cry out in pain. As soon as the mean-looking nurse realized that the old guy wouldn't be doing any talking, she turned her attention to me, and took up a pen and an information card.

"Name of patient?" she inquired.

"Gus," Lorraine piped up.

"Gus who?"

"Gus *Bore*," I invented on the spot.

"What kind of medical insurance does he have?"

"I don't have any," the old man grunted in an exhale. "Please, help me! Please get me a doctor!"

"Haven't you got Medicare?" the mean nurse pursued.

"Get him to a doctor!" I screamed at her. I wanted to reach out and grab her by the neck and bang her head on the desk. She took a close look at me, and I could see that she knew I meant business. She wanted to know who we were, so we told her we were his grand-children, and then she ordered us into the waiting room while she had the bozos in white uniforms roll the old man down the hall.

"We want to go with him," I said.

"That's against hospital rules," she said, and she sounded so secure about it I figured she wasn't lying. Besides, I knew it was better for her to think we were in the waiting room, because I'm an old hand at sneak-ing past nurses and going to visit whomever I want in hospitals. I had a cousin once who had his appendix out, and they said there was no visiting after eight o'clock. But I knew how to go up and down the back stairways and walk through the halls as though I was a plainclothes intern. Nobody asks you anything in hos-pitals if you look as though you belong there.

Lorraine and I decided we'd have to obey orders temporarily because the mean nurse really kept her eyes glued on us. We sat in the horrible waiting room, which had several junk-food machines, a couple of tele-phones, and these stupid little television sets that you could put a quarter in for an hour's worth of the boob tube.

I got Lorraine and myself hot chocolates with a cou-ple of quarters she had. She just sat on one of the benches sipping it and saying, "We killed him. We killed him. I know we killed him."

"He's not dead," I said.

"He's dying. I just know he's dying."

"There's a big difference between a stomachache and dying," I told her, and then I started to feel sick again myself. Maybe the marble pecan fudge had ptomaine in it, or botulism. After ten minutes I checked with the mean nurse and she told me to just go back and sit down. But I bugged her until she finally admitted the Colonel had been put in examination room number three. I decided to take up watch at the doorway to the waiting room, because from that point I could see all the way down the hall to where the examination rooms were. About a half hour later I saw an attendant roll the

Colonel out and start pushing him out of my sight down another hall. A doctor with a stethoscope came out of the room with two nurses behind him, and they all started heading my way. I signaled Lorraine, and we stopped the doctor right in the middle of the hall while the mean nurse kept yelling, "Get back in the waiting room! Get back in the waiting room!"

"Is he all right?" I asked the doctor.

"We're taking him upstairs now," the doctor said in a kind, professional voice.

"Can we take him home?" Lorraine asked.

"No. His system has had a terrible shock. We're going to have to run some tests. You're his grand-children?"

"Yes," I said.

"Then if you don't mind, please finish filling out the information on him. We're going to have to talk to your mother or father."

"Yes, sir," I said, and I was just getting ready to ask him another question when he wiped his nose on his sleeve and dashed off.

The mean-looking nurse seemed delighted. She had an *I-told-you-so* look on her face and Lorraine and I decided we had no other choice than to put down my address for the Colonel and my telephone number. We decided that if the hospital had to call it was better that they call my house, since Lorraine's mother would only think it was a crank and hang up.

"What's his birth date?" the mean nurse wanted to know.

"1906," I invented.

"Are you sure he has no medical protection whatso-ever?"

"I'm not sure," I said. "I just don't think so, but I'll check with my mother and father. They were out to-night playing bingo," I lied, "and then they were going to a chic cocktail party at the Waldorf-Astoria." The mean nurse grunted and started slipping another spe-cial sheet into the typewriter and began typing. Just then Lorraine nudged me and I turned from the infor-mation desk and looked down the hall. I couldn't be-lieve my eyes. There was the old man heading for us like a jogging ghost. He was dressed in a white hospital gown, and had just popped out of the elevator. I don't know why, but I felt he was up to something rather illegal, and I decided to keep saying crazy things to the nurse to distract her. "Oh, yes, and after the Waldorf-Astoria, they were going to go disco dancing at Studio 54, and then meet for a nightcap at the Plaza Hotel with Jane Fonda and the Archbishop of Canterbury." The nurse grunted and kept typing and mumbling things like "We're going to have to have his Social Security number. Who is his private physician? What is his religious preference?"

By this time the old man was practically up to us. He was taking these short rapid steps that made him look like a sandpiper. And he just zoomed by whispering very clearly to us, "Let's get the 3@#$% out of here!"

Lorraine looked dumbfounded, but I almost burst into laughter because I had never seen a more welcome or a funnier sight. The mean nurse was right in the middle of talking to us when she noticed us move quickly to become human crutches for this swiftly moving form which she recognized as a patient. She stood up from her desk and began to call after us, "Where do you *think* you're going? Sir! Sir! Come back here!"

We hit the automatic doors and they flung open. The Studebaker was waiting right where we had left it, and like the old pros that we were, within a flash we were in the front seat just as the mean nurse came out the door with a couple of confused attendants and another doctor who looked like a medicinal dwarf. The engine exploded. I threw the car into gear and we peeled rubber down the exit ramp, with a lot of people in white yelling.

"Where are your clothes" I asked.

"They got 'em the scavengers," the old man growled. "They got 'em!"

"I thought you *wanted* to go to the hospital," Lorraine reminded him. "You were in such a terrible pain."

"Yeah, well I'm not now. I just needed a little medicine, not a new home."

"Right," I said.

"You betcha," the old man agreed.

"Back to the house on the double?" I asked him.

He patted my knee again and smiled. "That's my boy! *That's my boy!*"

Now this next paragraph that I'm typing I'm not going to show to Lorraine until the book is over. She thinks I don't know that she's been writing pages on the side and hiding them, but I'm not stupid. I know she's been coming into the book closet and using the typewriter when I'm not here, and I found some of her pages hidden behind a set of *Silas Marner* on the top shelf right next to the one where I hide my cigarettes. I've got to tell you that when the old man slapped my knee and said "That's my boy!" it made me feel terrific inside. It made me feel terrific because my father never touches me, much less says "That's my boy." You see, my mother and father never even touch each other, which makes me wonder how on earth I ever was born. I figure it was just an accident—they both happened to be walking around the bedroom nude and they made a mistake and tripped. They had me so late in life they were too old and grouchy to be parents. I'm sure my mother would have been much happier giving birth to a bottle of Windex, and at that time my father would have preferred a keg of beer instead of a son. My parents never hug each other. At breakfast my father never reaches out and takes my mother's hand. My mother doesn't kiss my father when he comes home from work. We're a family of untouchables, and if you think that sort of thing doesn't rub off on the kids, you're crazy. My mother hates it if anybody even touches *themselves*. When I was three years old she caught me touching a sensuous part of my anatomy and threatened to slice it up like a pepperoni. She made me so nervous about my body that I could hardly walk, much less dance at a social gathering. I know Lorraine's case is similar to mine, because whenever we try to dance, the two of us are so awkward we practically fall down. Sometimes we even dance into other couples or crash into the wall. But once I realized what was going on, I tried to change all that. I took a good look at the teachers in my school. You could tell some of them had happy lives because they weren't afraid to hug you or

69

shake your hand, or say something nice and smile. Some of their faces didn't get all twisted up and frightened when something to do with sex came into the classroom conversation. When a kid is really frightened about touching other boys and girls and grown-ups, that's when I think a lot of problems come in. But what I'm really trying to say is that just about at this time I was beginning to think how nice it would be to be able to put my arms around Lorraine and start kissing her. (End of my humble secret paragraph.)

Ten

I can tell you one thing, by the end of Saturday John and I knew we had an incredible case history on our hands. We took the Colonel home and set him up in his chair and gave him a little cereal and milk. Gus had been barking loud and clear when we came up the driveway, and he seemed to really enjoy a couple of the boiled eggs we had made in the afternoon. The Colonel told us the whole sad story of how he hadn't been able to find Gus on the day he had to split from the town house, and we stayed with him until he fell asleep. The next morning we were over bright and early to fix him a little Sunday breakfast. We brought some bacon and a lot of other things we took out of our own kitchens, like a Belgian frying pan and a good spatula. The old man slept most of Sunday, which gave John and me plenty of time to talk about what we thought was going on. The names alone had been confusing. Sometimes I would call the old man Gus even though I knew now that Gus was the dog. And sometimes I would call the dog the Colonel. It took a whole lot of reconditioning for me to get it straight that the old man had really been a famous subway designer and no doubt once had a lot of money and had gone broke. Actually, the Colonel's story wasn't all that different from what had happened to Dolly Racinski—the custodial lunchroom woman at Franklin High—except Dolly had been more up front about it from the beginning. By the end of Dolly's first week pushing a broom in the lunchroom we knew her whole history. When she knew we were interested she came around to our table every third-period lunch and gave us each and every detail. She had never been married either but had fallen from a position of some importance. She had been an assistant dietician at Hill View Hospital on Staten Island when it was a TB sanatorium—but then they invented miracle drugs, and when TB disappeared they turned it into the Staten Island poorhouse and she was demoted to a sweeper. We had asked her one day why she didn't quit when they demoted her, and she said she would have lost her pension and she wasn't going to let the City cheat her out of it. We even asked her why she wore such large earrings and loud-colored dresses, and she said it was to cheer up the veterans, who used to make up most of the TB patients. Sometimes they had come to the hospital right from the war, and they always complimented her on her cheerful appearance. She told us half the fun of being a woman was to cheer people up and show them that life could be an upper. We didn't know it at the time, but all of these talents were going to come in handy pretty soon!

While the old man went through his trunk Sunday afternoon, John and I did our share of snooping and we saw a lot of tax bills. The Colonel hadn't paid real-estate taxes on the town house in years, and the only source of income we could find for him since he had retired was something called a Keogh Plan, where he was supposed to pay taxes on money which he himself had saved. Since he hadn't paid any of those taxes either there were a lot of bills from the IRS, so what we had now was a broke man who owed a lot of money.

Sunday night John and I treated the Colonel and Gus to pizza with extra cheese. Eventually, the Colonel fell asleep on the floor looking through the papers in the bottom of his trunk. We had to carry him to bed, or rather to chair, and we were very careful taking the chunk of blue crystal fossil from around his neck and placing it nearby so if he woke up, he wouldn't think it was stolen. All I knew was that everything was getting so complex we needed some adult to straighten it out. John and I began to feel helpless. We needed someone smarter than my mother and smarter than John's parents too. What we needed was someone who was really old.

Monday John and I agreed to meet during third-period lunch. We were still trying to figure out whether it would be more humane if we asked the Welfare

Department to help the old man, when Dolly Racinski made the mistake of pushing her broom right by us. Dolly, as always, wore her giant pom-pom rhinestone earrings, and was wearing a gold electric-colored dress under her smock.

"Hi, Dolly," John said. "How are you feeling today?"

"Lookin' up," she said perkily, "lookin' up!"

Some kids started throwing walnuts at her, so she went on a coffee break near this special table reserved for the custodial workers. I could tell by the look on John's face that we both had exactly the same idea. In a flash we were at her side. We just leveled with her about the Colonel. And even though she was only sixty years old, we knew from the other conversations with her that she was looking farther down the line and knew all about the way the United States government makes old people go broke. Finally we just got right to the point.

"Dolly, could you come over and at least meet the guy?"

"I'd *love* to," Dolly said immediately. I couldn't help noticing that she looked like she had just received a blind date for the prom four decades late. We knew she had never been married, but somehow we had just assumed she had gone out with a lot of veterans when she was at Hill View.

"You're great, Dolly, just great!" John said.

Dolly beamed and adjusted her right earring. "You two darlings are the only kids who make my work around here bearable. You appreciate a clean floor. The rest, they're like barbarians. For all the times you stood up for me and saved me from being hit with things, this is the least I could do for you."

After school we picked up some more food and got over to the Colonel's. He was sitting in a chair near the front door waiting for us. I felt sad because I knew he had done nothing all day but look forward to seeing us. I could just tell. John brought him his portable radio, and I brought a package of laundry I had taken home with me the night before. I made Gus two orders of scrambled eggs, which he just loved. He literally licked the plate clean and barked for more.

73

After dinner we decided it was better to break the news to the Colonel that Dolly Racinski would be coming over. We didn't want him to have a coronary the minute she walked in the door. He took the news a little paranoid at first, saying we really had turned him in to the IRS and that this Dolly Racinski was probably some agent assigned to fix his wagon. I even thought of calling Dolly and telling her to cancel the whole thing, but she arrived at eight o'clock and sparkled so much you'd think she was the midnight sun. John let her in, and I watched carefully as Dolly met the Colonel in the living room. We thought maybe the Colonel would yell at first, but to my surprise he looked like a bashful little boy. Dolly gave a great big *hello*, and the Colonel mumbled *hello* back. Then he excused himself and went upstairs to his bedroom.

"I'm sorry," I apologized to Dolly. "Maybe if we just give him a few minutes he'll come back on down."

"Don't worry about him," Dolly said. "I'm going *up*."

"You're going up?"

"Honey, leave it to me," she said, and went straight to the stairs. "We had cranks at Hill View, too."

"Should we go with you?" John wanted to know.

"This is just between us old folks." Dolly winked and disappeared up into the old man's bedroom.

Even Gus looked surprised; either that or he was blinded by Dolly's earrings and the electric-green dress that she was wearing that night. She also had a weird little handbag that was shaped like a doghouse. It was very cute, but it's the kind of thing you usually see an eight-year-old girl carry around, not a sixty-year-old lady. She was up there with the Colonel for over an hour. John remarked that maybe the two of them had died of angina. Then we heard some sounds and Dolly came down alone. She pulled us into the kitchen and spoke very dramatically.

"Oh, he's a *wonderful* man," Dolly said.

"He *is*, isn't he?" I said.

"I know just how he feels," Dolly sympathized. "He's been pushed around like so many of us. And he doesn't want to take it sitting down."

"I don't blame him," John said.

"Neither do I," Dolly agreed, "but he's too weak to fight back alone. He needs us. He needs you and me," Dolly emphasized. The force of her conviction caused her earrings to bounce against her cheeks. "But if you'll excuse me now, darlings, I've got to make the old boy some poached eggs."

John and I were so relieved that Dolly was taking over. It was a joy to watch her jangling around in the kitchen like a living laser beam. Her green dress flashed, and she bounced in and out under the lights as if she'd been sprayed with fluorescent paint. As she cracked those eggs and plopped them into boiling water, each one came out a perfect circle. For the first time in several days it seemed like everything was going to be all right. It was only when I got a closer look at Dolly, I noticed a distinct sense of panic in her eyes. I may not be a psychologist yet, but I'll tell you one thing—I can tell if a person is making believe that everything is all right when it isn't.

"Something's wrong, isn't it, Dolly?" I said.

"Lorraine, whatever are you talking about?" Dolly plopped the eggs onto a piece of toast. "Everything's just fine."

"Why did the Colonel cry out in pain the other night? Why did we have to take him to the hospital? Why didn't he stay?" I asked.

Dolly began to hum and spoke between musical passages. "The Colonel has *diverticulosis*," she explained.

"Oh, my God," I said. I didn't know what diverticulosis was, but it sounded fatal.

"It's just a little intestinal condition, and all that fudge he ate caused an attack, that's all." Dolly was very reassuring. "But don't you worry, my little honeys, I'll work out the right diet for him. I know what's best for him." Suddenly there was a sound in the kitchen doorway, and we turned to see the Colonel.

"Who *are* you really?" the Colonel snapped at Dolly.

"We told you," John said. "This is Dolly. She was just talking to you for an hour in your bedroom."

"Well, she's forgettable," the Colonel stated.

"Why are you being so rude?" I asked.

"Shush!" Dolly said. "I can take care of myself,

75

Lorraine." Then she carried the plate of poached eggs right past the old man and set it down on a small table in the dining room. "Don't you jump down my throat, you old buzzard. I came here to help."

"Yeah?" the old guy wheezed. "Well, I was upstairs thinking about it, and I decided that you really came here just to make fun of me."

"Excuse me, Colonel," I said, "but now you *are* acting a little paranoid."

"I am not. If she's here to start cooking poached eggs and playing canasta with me, I'm not interested."

Dolly chuckled. "I didn't come here to play canasta, or even strip poker if that's your game. Besides, if you think you're going to scare me off, I want you to know the old goats at Hill View used to bellyache just like you. I find it charming. Now sit down and eat your dinner."

The Colonel gave her a good feisty look, then focused in on the eggs. In a flash he sat down and started tearing into them like he had into the fudge. Dolly gave us a great big wink. "That's a good boy," she said to the Colonel. "That's a very good boy."

"You're not my doctor, you know," came the reply.

"I know it," Dolly seconded as she gave the old man a paper towel for a napkin.

"You probably think I'm crazy, don't you?" the Colonel wanted to know.

"If you can count five stones and know your name, then I don't think you're crazy. That's always been my rule for nuts." Then she reached into her doghouse-shaped pocketbook and took out a half pint of blackberry brandy. "This will really hit the spot," she said, pouring the Colonel a small shot.

The Colonel grunted and took a sip.

"Are you sure that's good for him?" I asked.

"Of course it is," Dolly replied. "It's organic."

It got so it felt as if we were butting into Dolly and the Colonel's private little party, so John and I went out and did the dishes. Later on Dolly served ice cream for dessert.

"Tastes like homemade," the Colonel grunted.

Dolly took the Colonel's hand at that point and gave

76

it a big squeeze. Then she turned to us and said, "Oh, my darlings, this has been wonderful, hasn't it? I haven't enjoyed myself this much in years. Everything's lookin' up, lookin' up." Her pom-pom earrings flickered now as though they were on fire. John and I decided it would be a good idea if he and I took a walk and let the two of them be alone.

"You kids are swell," Dolly said to that idea. "You kids are just swell."

The night was getting rather cool, and a fog was coming in off the ocean and we could actually see it ducking under the Verrazano Bridge. John took my hand and we walked the whole length of Howard Avenue, past the convent and the whole string of fancy houses perched on the cliffs. We even went past the house where Eileen Farrell, the famous opera singer, used to live, and farther down there was an old house where Dame Sybil Leek did a television program about spooks in an old stucco house. I don't know why, but I love to walk by famous people's houses. The most famous person's house I ever walked past was Phyllis Whitney's house, which happened to be in St. George, but on a street much higher up than where the Colonel's town house was. I loved reading all the mysteries she wrote. And one time she came to my high school and gave a great speech where she told a fantastic story about somebody and then at the end of the story we found out that the somebody was somebody famous like Einstein or Mary Baker Eddy. As we walked, John did a lot of talking about the Colonel and Dolly, and how strange old people are. He thought the two of them acted like two-year-old babies when they meet each other for the first time in supermarket baskets. Little babies wave to each other and smile and reach out even though they've never met before.

Right here I'm going to start another paragraph I'm not going to let John read until we're finished writing the book; then I'll stick it in. As we were walking along I wasn't listening to John's babblings. I was more focused in on the fact that he was holding my hand and at least four times I just wanted to stop, put my arms around him and kiss him on the lips. Sometimes I think a girl has to do something like that, because some boys are really slow. I also have a theory that there are a lot of homely girls who get very good-looking boys because they are aggressive and make up for good-looking boys' shyness. There's a girl, Peggy Lamberti, who really is physically a disaster, even so much as having bumps on her nose. But she goes after all the shy terrific-looking guys and gets them. She has what's called personality. That means that she can play the piano, compliment the boys a mile a minute, and dance in these skirts that flare out. In situations where other girls would be in tears, Peggy laughs delightfully. The more John talked about the Colonel and Dolly, the more my mind drifted to every thought I ever had about love and sex. Of course there was a lot of information in my head about love and sex because recently the public-school system on Staten Island canceled a big Sex and Love Information Conference that was supposed to be held under the auspices of the Mental Health Society. The principals of the schools decided it was too risky, so the kids decided to chip in and support the conference anyway outside of school. It was a terrific day, and I learned a lot of things from all the various discussions I attended. I don't know why, but a lot of stuff from that conference came barging through my head, like the two best seminars, called, "Sex: Ready or Not!" and "Rape—It Can Happen to You." Then there was another panel where they gave you a list of a lot of things that kids should think about in order to find out what kind of person they are. Some of the questions you were supposed to ask yourself were, "If someone gave you five hundred dollars, what would you do with it?" and "What characteristics would you want most in a best friend?" There were a lot of weird classes in the conference, too. One was called "In Defense of Virgins," which basically made the point that after boys go through a very passionate period in high school, they seem to be less obsessive about carnal wishes later on. I had to laugh at one session I went to called "Why Sex Education Belongs in the Home." If that ever went on in my home, my mother would shoot me with a bazooka. The conference also had other workshops for mothers and fathers. They were very provocative and called things like "What to Do If Your Teenager Is Having Sex" and "You Can't Stop Your Child from Having Sex." Another thing I got out of the conference was this theory about the ABC's of responsible sex. It said if you could just remember that "A" stands for abstinence, "B" is for baby, and "C" is for contraception, then everything would work out all right in life. And I remembered another thing in a pamphlet. They said that when a boy takes a girl home, all he really expects is a couple of kisses. And for a lot of boys this is all they can really handle comfortably. This pamphlet says that a boy is really relieved when a girl doesn't give in to his complaint about not getting more on a date. But I think this pamphlet was printed several years ago. They also had a wonderful poster they gave out that showed a doctor, a construction worker, and a bricklayer. Three tough-looking men, all of whom had gigantic bellies. Underneath the picture it said, "Would you be more careful if it was *you* who got pregnant?" But I guess the fact that really impressed me was that over fifty percent of kids my age do go all the way. Well at least that leaves about another fifty percent who are probably in the same boat I am. Maybe it's not a better boat, and maybe it's not a worse boat; maybe it's just the right boat for some kids. Sometimes, though, the more I read in the psychology books and magazines about sex, the less appealing it is. And the more I learn about it in all the sex manuals they hand out, the more scary it is. Sometimes I wish schools could just teach sex ignorance courses so I could spend more time being myself and less time worrying about what everybody else is doing. Anyway all I'm really trying to tell you is what was on my mind. I just felt like expressing to John that I thought we should be closer, so I put my arm around his waist and moved closer to him as we went by Eileen Farrell's house. I could tell I made John lose his train of thought for a moment. He was talking about what a kind lady Dolly Racinski was. And I knew he was taken off guard by my action. I was terrified that I might have gone too far and John would just brush me away like a leper, not because he hated me, but because his feelings weren't growing like mine. After a terrible silence, he put his arm around me and resumed talking about Dolly. My fingers on his waist got so nervous I thought he would yell at me for causing vibrations to his bellybutton. Although he didn't say anything about our new proximity, his hand rubbed my right shoulder softly as though telling me *It's okay*. Somehow I heard my mother's voice in my head at just that moment screaming one of her favorite things, like "You watch out for boys. They're all dirty and only want one thing." (This is the end of my secret paragraph.)

By the time we got back to the old house, Dolly had moved two chairs onto the sun porch and bundled the old man up to look at the stars.

"That's it," we heard Dolly yelling. "That's the Big Dipper," she said, pointing up toward the moon. "I can only find the Big Dipper and the North Star."

"I only know Betelgeuse," the Colonel muttered.

Dolly let out a squeal of joy when she saw us coming up the front walk. She dashed down toward the steps, her earrings ablaze.

"We're going to Atlantic City!" She beamed. "The Colonel has always wanted to see Atlantic City!" Dolly and the Colonel laughed joyously and even Gus began to bark. John and I didn't know what had gone on while we were gone, but one thing was for sure—nobody on that porch acted as though they had diverticulosis!

Eleven

We all tucked the Colonel into his chair and had a few more good laughs before he fell asleep for the night with Gus plopped at his feet like a rug. Then we walked Dolly home to Castleton Avenue, and Lorraine kept quizzing her whether someone who had been screaming in pain from diverticulosis should really be going to Atlantic City. Dolly kept stressing that was *what the Colonel wanted*. But there was something weird in her tone again, as though she was holding some secret back from us. I didn't think anything about it until the next morning when Lorraine called me at seven A.M. to say she was talking about diverticulosis with her mother, and her mother said that diverticulosis was a big word that could mean a lot of things. In general it meant that there was some kind of obstruction growing in the Colonel's intestines, and if he had screamed in pain like Lorraine described, then the Colonel must be in pretty rough shape. Mrs. Jensen had said there are usually operations and things that can straighten it out, but if the condition has gone too far, a person could croak from it. I told her I really wanted to go to Atlantic City. I thought it would be a lot of fun.

"John," Lorraine said, "a man who was screaming in pain, like the Colonel was, can't be in any condition to take a drive like that."

"I heard you can really scream in pain from gas," I told her. And I personally gave Dolly a vote of confidence that she must know what she's doing. If she says the Colonel should go to Atlantic City, then he should go to Atlantic City.

We got over to the house before nine o'clock, and Dolly had already arrived and was cooking breakfast for the Colonel and Gus. We told them we had over thirty-seven dollars between us. I had borrowed twenty from

Bore, and Lorraine had broken open a piggy bank for another seventeen bucks.

"That's all right," Dolly said, "I've got a few dollars, and the Colonel is going to sell his silver dollars."

"Oh, I don't think you should do that," Lorraine said.

"Why not?" the Colonel asked. "Didn't you ever hear that expression, *You can't take it with you?*" He let out a little chuckle. But I happened to notice Dolly's eyes get a sudden sad look to them, and again I felt as though there was some sort of secret going on that Lorraine and I didn't know about. And then for some reason we were quiet for a while finishing all the preparations. Dolly had already called in sick, said she wouldn't be pushing her broom around at school today. Lorraine and I decided to plain *cut* our classes and face the consequences afterward. The sky was just too beautiful to worry about something like school attendance. You could look right out the back of the house and see straight to the Blue Mountains of Jersey and the huge oil tanks about forty miles away looming like steaming monuments against the New Jersey skyline. Lorraine had borrowed a few of her mother's nursing journals, and she was surreptitiously flipping through those as a sort of handy reference guide in case the Colonel had another attack on the way. Except for her one lapse into a quick downer, Dolly was the only one who didn't seem worried. She was even baking biscuits and had armed herself with butter and jam and a thermos of milk. I guess the saddest thing was watching Gus's face as he began to realize he wasn't going with us. I pulled the Studebaker out of the garage, and as everyone piled in Gus barked like a trouper from inside the house.

"Are you sure you don't want him to come?" Dolly asked.

"No," the Colonel said. "It wouldn't be fair to lock him up in the car while we walked along the Boardwalk. I'm sure they don't let dogs on the Boardwalk and surely not on the beach. Besides, I lost him once and I don't want to lose him again."

I personally thought it was terrific that the Colonel wanted to drive straight to the Silver Exchange on Bay Street. I could see that Lorraine wasn't happy about the

Colonel selling his collection, but when she saw that his one hundred twenty-three silver dollars were turned into over six hundred dollars she changed her mind and realized why he had really wanted the trunk. That was a lot of money for a guy who had no cash. And he could even take that and rent a decent room somewhere and be able to eat for a few months, but it wouldn't be enough to pay taxes with, I didn't think.

By noon we had the top down on the Studebaker, and I was driving like a movie star over the Outerbridge Crossing and zooming down into Perth Amboy to pick up the Garden State Parkway. "Atlantic City, here we come," everybody was singing. "Atlantic City, here we come."

"Oh, I love it," Dolly said. "Things are lookin' up, really lookin' up!" She looked ecstatic in the backseat with the Colonel, smoothing out her blue electric dress and checking to make sure her tight little pile of white curls still sat sprayed and firm on top of her head. Sometimes the Colonel would turn and look at her and I noticed in the rearview mirror that he looked a bit like a parrot in profile—a very alert, happy parrot whenever his eyes fell on Dolly. He was wearing a pullover sweater and a turtleneck with a little tear on a seam just above the spot where his fossil medallion swung back and forth, creating a semicircle of blue flashing that matched Dolly's dress.

"I just love it when you smile," Dolly told the Colonel. "When you smile your eye strength improves. Of course you must eat carrots too. Tomorrow I'll bake you my grandmother's favorite country carrot cake."

"I hate carrots," the Colonel said factually. In fact, he did complain a lot on the trip, but you could tell it was just his personality. He was really having a good time. He'd get real excited whenever we'd pass over train tracks. The only thing he didn't seem to like was when there were tracks that had been abandoned and grass had grown between the railroad ties. He also spent a good deal of time complaining about all the quarters that the toll booths were eating up. "Boy, the Garden State Parkway really gobbles up your quarters," he said about a dozen times. But Dolly didn't pay any attention to him and just dipped into his pocket regularly to pass the money forward to me. At one point steam began to shoot out from under the hood of the Studebaker, threatening to turn us all into succulent roasts. It got so it was almost impossible to breathe. But we finally made it to a gas station called the Lucky Seven Mine Fill-'er-Up Stop, which was supposed to be a haven for truck drivers with block-long trailers. I got out and checked under the hood. It was only a loose water hose, and in no time I had the radiator filled with cold water. Dolly didn't budge from the Colonel's side in the backseat. She let him use her as a pillow while he dozed off—which looked kind of cute. It dawned on me that I had never once seen my father use my mother for a pillow. If he had I'm sure she would have tried to Lysol his head.

I bought us some coffee and donuts, since we had already stopped. And at one point Dolly slipped out from under the Colonel and went to the ladies' room with Lorraine. When they came back I noticed that Dolly had helped fix Lorraine's hair into a French twist and put makeup on parts of her face that I had never seen made up before.

"Isn't she a beauty?" Dolly asked me. "Isn't she a beauty?"

"Oh, yeah, a real beauty," I said.

"But makeup isn't the thing that makes a girl beautiful," Dolly added. "John knows that, don't you?"

"Do I?" I asked.

"Oh, yes, I can see it in your eyes," she said slipping back under the dozing Colonel. "You kids are swell! You kids are just *swell!*" she kept saying.

I started the car again and before you knew it we had thrown a couple of more quarters into the toll booths on the Garden State. Somewhere beyond the Asbury Park turnoff the Colonel snored so loud he woke himself up. And he didn't doze off again on the whole trip, which had to be due to Dolly's vivaciousness. Most of the time the motor was making so much noise I couldn't hear everything the Colonel and Dolly were saying. But they were laughing and waving to people in other cars.

Then at one point he started grilling Dolly about the Game of Life, and she did all the things he told her about closing her eyes, and it looked like she was having a ball. Dolly said the road she could see in her imagination was a terrific beautiful highway and she said she found a key that looked like it belonged to a church door, and picked it up to save it. And when she found a cup, she said it was made of beautiful porcelain, and she sipped from it and had tea biscuits. And her Tree of Sex turned out to be a beautiful pear tree with doves sitting on all the branches. When it got time for her to imagine the wall at the end of her Road of Life, I slowed the car down to quiet the motor. I didn't want to miss this. The Colonel told her how the wall reached for eternity in all directions, and in the mirror I watched the expression on Dolly's face change from great joy to incredible seriousness.

"What do you do at the wall?" the Colonel asked, his eyes glowing with anticipation.

"I fall down on my knees and kiss it," Dolly said.

I got a terrible chill when she said that, and I think even the Colonel was shocked. When he told her that it was the Wall of Death, she explained that she really was a very religious person so she thought that might explain why she wasn't so afraid of dying. Actually all that talk about death in the backseat was getting a little frightening. I think it even rattled Dolly, because she kept checking her own face in the mirror of her compact. I tried to keep my eye on the real road of life, which at the moment was a very busy strip in New Jersey that was going to end at Exit 40. When we got off, there were huge signs pointing toward the Boardwalk. We passed a Ramada Inn with a mural of a huge bull that had been painted on the entire side of the building facing Atlantic Avenue. The bull was huffing and puffing at the street, and there was the cross of life through his nose. It was a very macabre greeting.

"Here we are, gang," I said.

"Where?" Lorraine asked.

"We must have made a wrong turn," the Colonel said.

"Nope, this is it," Dolly exclaimed. "This is Atlantic City. I used to come here all the time as a kid and eat saltwater taffy and ride the Whip. I love the sound of the waves crashing." Then she became more practical. "It said *valet parking* down close to the Boardwalk. It's not every day a knight of Sweden comes to this town." Right near the Boardwalk was a very large building, and sure enough, two valet guys came running out and helped us out of the car like we were royalty. Then one of them who looked like he was stoned got behind the wheel and the Studebaker burned rubber as it was taken up this high ramp away from us.

"You want the *special* restaurant?" The other valet guy winked. "You bet," Dolly said.

I must admit there was something rather elegant about Dolly and the Colonel as they walked together behind the guy. And I found it was so sweet that he was trying as hard as he could not to use her as a crutch. Her dress swayed in the breeze like a blue parachute. And the Colonel's pullover did not match his trousers or turtleneck, but that didn't matter. The way they clung to each other, you'd have thought they were the Prince and Princess of Tasmania. I thought it was better that way because it probably would blind them to how ugly Atlantic City really was. Lorraine and I couldn't quite adjust to the fact that this "special restaurant" looked like nothing more than a converted old office building that had been temporarily saved from atomic detonation. Hundreds of tiny windows and shades decorated the exterior of the building, which made it about as glamorous as a condemned law school. There was something about the new marble facade and the automatic doors with the electronic surveillance system that didn't go with the rest of the building. It seemed like a big phony tourist trap just waiting to fleece anybody who walked into it. Inside there was a lot of color, as though a rainbow had gone berserk, and I began to think maybe it was making up for what the outside lacked. The valet guy put his hand out for a tip, frowned at the dollar bill Dolly put in it, and opened a final door. To our shock, the "special restaurant" turned out to be a giant gambling casino! I had heard so much about casinos and I thought it would be the most chic place for a kid to be, but when I looked around it seemed like everybody was pretty old and wearing toupees, or else they looked like they were all out from the poorhouse desperately hoping to make a million. What there *was* was a great big feeling of doom in the air. A good portion of the people around us were carrying little black promotional T-shirts that proclaimed the virtues of the Florida Mortuary Union, which was having a convention at a nearby hotel. Most of them were lining up at the cheap slot machines, which made me think that they weren't doing so well in the embalming business. There was no bounce or excitement. It seemed like all of them were zombies even when their machines came up winners. Just when I thought Dolly and the Colonel would want to turn around and exit in horror, something amazing happened. The Colonel gave Lorraine and me a hundred-dollar bill. We almost died.

"We can't take it," Lorraine said. "We should get out of here."

"*I'll* take it," I said. "This place looks like fun!"

"Live it up, kids," the Colonel said. "Live it up!"

Dolly nodded that it was okay, but I could see Lorraine look at me suspiciously when I pocketed the hundred, and I tried to change the subject. The look on Lorraine's face was so disturbed you'd think we had come down there planning to gamble. Not only that, you'd think that we were going to gamble for the Colonel's life and future. But he had a few hundred more. It wasn't going to be life or death. And he wanted us to have it. But what he seemed to really want was for me and Lorraine to go off by ourselves and leave him and Dolly alone. We took the hint and everybody agreed to meet back in front of the Rendezvous Lounge and Oyster Bar in an hour and a half—just so we could check on each other and see if we wanted to walk down the Boardwalk at that point.

"I'll take my fifty dollars," Lorraine said right off the bat as soon as we were alone.

"I thought you didn't want the money."

"Well, I *do*."

I changed the hundred dollars and gave Lorraine her fifty. But I knew she just wanted to hold on to the fifty so I wouldn't blow it. I could see she was really nervous. I just took her hand and we walked around the place sizing it up. We watched them play craps at a few tables. One guy was rolling a lot of sevens and yelled, "Yahooo!" and eventually the whole table was yelling, "Yahooo!" It looked like he was winning a whole lot. But except for that table the whole crowd seemed extra dull. If it hadn't been for croupiers shouting out numbers at the roulette tables every once in a while, and some big brute running the Wheel of Fortune booming like a cannon, you would have thought we were in a tomb. Nobody spoke to anybody else, which made me realize we were in the company of diehard gamblers. We decided to play a few of the slot machines, and it took over an hour before they devoured five dollars worth of nickels. By that time there were so many lemons, cherries, and oranges rolling in my head, I thought I was on a psychedelic fruit trip. At one point we were surprised when we found Dolly and the Colonel sitting at a blackjack table. They were perched on these high stools looking very regal. Dolly was the only one really turning over cards, and we saw that she won a hand. The two of them howled and the Colonel kept patting Dolly's hand. They were both so sophisticated. Dolly sat adjusting her ashtray six or seven times, smoking a very long filter tip and fiddling with their betting chips. Lorraine and I stood back far enough so they wouldn't see us, and at one point the Colonel placed a bet on the spot next to Dolly.

He was dealt a ten and a five, so I figured he was certain to be a loser. After a moment Dolly screamed out, referring to the dealer, "He went over twenty-one, my darling. You *won!*"

"And *you* got blackjack," the Colonel said, like a surprised little boy.

"Oh, you're right," Dolly said. Then she hugged him. Dolly even shouted to the other people at the blackjack table. You could tell some of them thought she was a nuisance, but a few people who were looking particularly sad seemed glad at the sound of her infectious laugh. You could tell everyone was impressed by her earrings, which were without a doubt the brightest thing in the whole casino.

By this time Lorraine and I weren't as uptight, so we walked down toward the slot machines again where people were lined up three and four deep like cattle about to be slaughtered. I started to take notice of one machine that was lit up and ringing as it spit quarters out. I thought it was a very interesting comment about civilization. That so many people would flock to this place to yank on all these machine handles in an atmosphere of red velour walls and fake gold decorations. I just got to feeling like we really were all one big herd, and that frightened me so much I bumped into a waitress who was serving free drinks. Her name was Number 43 and she asked me if I wanted a drink. I told her I'd go for a scotch on the rocks and my girl friend would like a Tab.

"You don't drink scotch," Lorraine chastised me after Number 43 left. "Besides, if there's a raid you'll be up on *two* charges."

"She'd know we were kids if I ordered a Coke," I explained. By this time I noticed that all the workers in the casino had numbers instead of names. What a horrible world! Can you imagine people going around saying, "Hello, Number 0." "How are you today, Number 8?" Finally Number 43 came back and Lorraine took big gulps of her Tab. I took a sip of my scotch. I'd always thought it was amazing how much like Mercurochrome it tasted. I think if you really have class you order something like a milkshake with a shot of brandy in it, or Dry Sack on the rocks. After a couple more sips of the scotch, I thought it would be a good idea if I switched to a horse's neck or a Singapore sling. There are some benefits you get from having a father who was an alcoholic, and one of them is knowing the most picturesque ways to tie a load on.

"John, you know what you were like when you used to drink," Lorraine reminded me.

"Don't worry," I said. "I'm not going to get stoned."

After a few minutes Lorraine wanted to check the

Rendezvous Lounge and Oyster Bar, but I told her we still had a lot of time to go before meeting Dolly and the Colonel. She started to bellyache about how she really didn't feel secure enough to start playing one of the real games. I could see she was almost afraid to talk to anyone, and absolutely terrified about a raid. Finally Lorraine broke down and got ten dollars' worth of nickels. I could see she was finally getting the feel of things. But her philosophy was, just because she had some money she didn't want to spend all of it right away. She still insisted on playing only the nickel slots.

I was playing the twenty-five-cent slots and got behind an oversized woman with short hair who kept turning around and smiling, but she wouldn't let me get at the machines. She kept plugging quarters in five at a time. By the time ten minutes passed I was still standing there. I felt like giving her a karate chop on the back of the neck. I couldn't wait to get at that particular machine, because I felt good vibes about it. At that point a middle-aged couple passed by and I heard the man say to his wife, "And here, Helen, is where the poor people line up." His wife replied, "Well, that's what we are," and got right in with the rest of us.

At last the corpulent dame in front of me turned around and said, "That's it. I'm wiped out. Twenty-five dollars and I didn't even get three lemons."

I zipped in like a ferret and started sticking quarters into the machine. I could feel the lady's eyes burning into my back. One of the quarters got stuck halfway down and I felt embarrassed.

"Pull the handle a little more," the lady coached me.

I did as she said and suddenly the winner's light lit up and the machine started coughing quarters out like there was no tomorrow—ten, twenty, fifty dollars' worth of quarters.

"Lorraine, Lorraine," I called out, jumping up and down. She was speechless watching me. The fat lady wasn't so speechless. "Those are my quarters you're winning," she said and took off in tears.

"I feel sorry for her," Lorraine said.

"So do I," I admitted, filling a paper cup with all the loot. I was so excited by now, I wanted to do cartwheels. I wanted to scream out loud, "I won! I won!" I put in another quarter and this time I won three quarters. The time after that I got two lemons and a hammer and won fifteen quarters. By then I got so daring I started playing five quarters at a time in the machine. And I heard Lorraine's little voice in my ear beginning to pray along with me. But her prayer had a slightly different twist on it.

"Please win. *Win for the Colonel*," Lorraine kept saying.

Sometimes the machine listened, but more often than not it didn't. Nevertheless I kept feeding the machine and some man next to me won two thousand quarters on his machine. But there was absolutely no expression on his face bacause he was with the mortuary convention. Finally, I decided the whole thing was a losing proposition and I took my quarters to the cashier and had her stick them into this automatic counting machine. I found that I hadn't really lost anything. In fact I came out about seventy-five cents ahead. Then I took Lorraine's hand and dragged her to the big Wheel of Fortune. The spirit suddenly moved me, and I plopped down a fifty-dollar bill.

"Money plays," the guy running the thing yelled out. I was going to stick it on a twenty-to-one space, but I decided the five-to-one space was risky enough. The little spinner went around and around, ticking in and out of the little slots. It took a long time to slow down, and it passed a lot of five-to-one slots. Our hopes went up and down until miraculously it stopped solidly between two pegs clearly marked five-to-one. I let out a scream so loud eight hundred people turned around. "I won!" I kept screaming. "I won!" Two hundred and fifty smackers I got, and I was so bananas I couldn't stay in one spot anymore. I took a twenty-dollar bill and slapped it right in the hand of the guy running the thing.

"What are you doing?" Lorraine wanted to know.

"*Tipping*."

"Are you crazy?"

"That's how it's done," I told her.

"Holy cow!" Lorraine moaned, shaking her head back

and forth in disbelief. "Holy cow!" I finally recovered and was about to try again when we heard another "Yahooo!" come tearing across the room. We recognized Dolly's scream, but it took us a while to locate her. We listened carefully for the next "Yahoo!" and found her with the Colonel at a different blackjack table where the minimum bet was ten dollars instead of five dollars.

"Oh, my darlings," Dolly said. "We're *four thousand dollars* ahead! I can't believe it! I'm so happy!"

Dolly got down off the stool and grabbed Lorraine and they began to dance in the aisle. They were just jumping up and down, and I was more thrilled than either of them. I could just smell the four thousand dollars as we all marched on the cashier's booth and turned in the chips. Dolly held the Colonel's arm the whole way and hugged it tightly against her body.

We made our way out of the joint. I tipped the valet guy a five and asked if there was another "special restaurant" around, and they told me there were three others down at the south end of the Boardwalk. Dolly's ecstasy and her electric blue swirl dress caught everyone's attention. We were almost up onto the Boardwalk when the Colonel suddenly stopped. I thought he might be in pain, but it was just the opposite. He wanted to go into a jewelry shop.

"What for?" Dolly wanted to know.

"I want to buy you a diamond," the Colonel wheezed.

Dolly started to cry. She opened her little doghouse purse, took out a handkerchief, and dabbed at her eyes. "Oh, my darling," she said. "I don't need a diamond. All I need is to know that you've got a decent roof over your head and three square meals a day. This money is going right into your bank account, and it's going to be ready for you whenever you need it." She beamed.

"But I want to buy you a ring."

"No, my darling," Dolly said, "not now."

"If I could afford it, you'd be covered with diamonds," the Colonel said, "*covered*."

Dolly grabbed his hand and pulled him right past the jewelry store and up onto the Boardwalk. It was really great that the old guy wanted to lay a diamond on

Dolly. The only thing shiny I ever saw my father buy for my mother was a soup pot.

We weren't on the Boardwalk two minutes before we were almost knocked down by a bearded man wearing glasses, a white apron, and a paper chef's hat. He was walking around in an absolute daze as though he'd had marijuana brownies for breakfast.

"He's an omen," Lorraine said. "That man is an omen."

The guy disappeared into the crowd and we pushed our way farther on down the Boardwalk. It was populated with a bunch of ancient-looking old ladies who were attacking every snack stand in sight. Then there was this open bus contraption that went up and down the Boardwalk on little rubber wheels. And it was filled with the saddest-looking old faces in the world. I called it a geriatric perambulator. One woman was walking around in her bare feet and I couldn't understand how she wasn't crippled with splinters. The wood on the Boardwalk was in a complete state of disrepair and looked ready to topple over into the ocean. The whole scene made me doubt my basic belief that reality is only a crutch for those people who are afraid to face science fiction. The Colonel and Dolly held hands, and the Colonel lit Dolly's filter-tip cigarettes. She fed him sesame-seed crackers, and she bought some popcorn. Her miniature doghouse purse seemed to be loaded with a lot of surprise goodies. She offered me a Tiger's Milk Health Bar.

The next "special restaurant" was pretty far down the Boardwalk, and we passed a lot of old stores and fast-food stands. There was a lot of window-shopping to do, and a saltwater taffy store. Another place was called the "Earring Tree," where they sold a lot of weird jewelry. Halfway down the Boardwalk we turned and went through this little teepee village, but we were chased out. All along the Boardwalk they seemed to sell everything from cameras to iron-on shirts. And we passed Madame Charlotte's Temple of Knowledge, and she was waving at us to come in for a phrenology reading. It was only a dollar.

"Should we give it a try?" Lorraine asked.

"I'm not going to pay any gypsy to feel the bumps on my head."

Then there was a carpenter peddling up and down the Boardwalk making signs while you wait. He looked like the type who worked part-time as a beautician. I was going to ask the Colonel if he'd like to make a sign commemorating our trip here, but I decided it would cut into our gambling time.

The sun was shining overhead as we walked into the second "special restaurant." The outside of this building was covered with a lot of lopsided sheets of shiny gold plastic. It looked like a cross between a Chinese pagoda and a jukebox. The inside was different too. At least they had a sense of humor, and looked like they must have really paid the cops off. The cashiers and dealers were all dressed in ruffled shirts and tuxedo vests. There were different kinds of music coming from all parts of the huge floor. Actually the spirit in the place was sort of intoxicating. Dolly and the Colonel were immediately swept away by the atmosphere.

"Let's have some lunch," Dolly suggested.

"I'm not hungry," I said. "Besides, don't you want to gamble some more?"

"Not really," Dolly said. "Do you, honey?"

"No," the Colonel admitted. "I'm just worried about the money."

"Darlings, would you mind holding it for us?" Dolly asked.

"*No*," I said right off the bat.

"You've got tight pockets on your jeans," Dolly said, "and if you just shove all the bills down deep nobody will be able to get them out. Around here they steal purses and once in a while they will hit old people over the head. I would feel safer if you kept it for us."

"Maybe it would be better if *you* just hung on to it, Dolly," Lorraine suggested.

"Nonsense," I said. "It's much safer with me." Dolly gave me forty-three one-hundred-dollar bills, which looked like a mafia bankroll.

"Do you need another hundred dollars?" the Colonel asked Lorraine and me.

"No," I said. We'd made a few dollars too.

"Yahoo!" Dolly yelled. "The Colonel and I are just going to get a little lunch at the Calypso Lounge until you come back in about an hour. Is it a deal?"

"You got it!" I said.

"*I really think you should hold the money,*" Lorraine repeated to Dolly.

"John is big and strong," Dolly stated. "Nobody's going to take it away from him."

Lorraine looked dubious, and as we walked away, Dolly was calling after us, "You kids are swell! You kids are just swell!"

I suppose I should have known the minute they gave me all that money to hold that maybe it really wasn't a very good idea. I really had no intention of gambling with it. I had over two hundred fifty dollars of my own from the last winnings, and there was no reason in the world why I'd have to dip into anybody else's money. I guess it was just the feeling that Dolly was the one with the lucky fingers who seemed to know her way around a blackjack table.

"Let's just have a soda and walk around," Lorraine suggested.

"After we play a few cards," I said. I finally found a blackjack table with only a few people at it, but the minimum was fifty dollars. Looking back now, I think it would have been better if I had waited for a five-dollar minimum, but they were all so crowded. I liked the luxury of space at this one particular one, and I felt that Lady Luck was calling to me. Lorraine said she was going over to the cashier's window to get some nickels to play the slot machines behind me. She decided sitting at a blackjack table made her much too nervous, because she definitely wasn't going to bet any fifty-dollar minimum and the dealer told her straight off that all the stools were reserved for players, not onlookers. Off to the right the Calypso Lounge was in view, and we could see Dolly and the Colonel seated at a dimly lit table drinking some exotic-looking drinks in a big coconut. For a guy who had intestinal problems, he didn't seem to care for some reason. When it came to eating and drinking that day, he was more like a guy going to the electric chair and having one heck of a final meal.

At least this place had a band, which was playing something like the "Anniversary Waltz." It was all sort of tender and romantic, especially with the old-fashioned music. There was a rock band down at the other end, but we could hardly hear the beat from where I was sitting.

I lost a couple of bets, then I put down a hundred dollars. I have a theory that you should always start out big and then work down to smaller bets. That way if you're going to win a lot, at least you'll win it at the beginning, and if you lose a lot then you can just play for peanuts and have fun afterward.

"John," Lorraine was at my side cautioning, "do you think you should really bet so much?"

"Start big, win big," I said.

"Did Dolly tell you her system of playing in multiples of five?" Lorraine asked.

"I know that system," I said. "It takes too long."

Before she could say another word, I placed my last fifty-dollar chip in my betting spot. I was so nervous I asked for more cards than I should have and went over twenty-one. The dealer hit twenty-one and everyone at the table lost anyway, so I didn't feel so bad. So now I was down to my original twenty-dollar bill that I had borrowed from my father. But somehow, something went berserk in my head and I just couldn't bear starting small again. It's like some disciple of the devil just grabbed my hand and thrust it into my left pocket to pull out the wad of C-notes. I peeled off five, knowing I couldn't possibly lose it. I had lost four hands in a row and I was really due to win big.

"What are you doing?" Lorraine asked, her eyes looking as though I was about to commit a heinous crime.

"Just getting my money back," I said.

"John, are you crazy? It's not your money."

"I'm just *borrowing* it," I explained.

"John, get away from that table."

"Lorraine, stop it please. Don't worry about it—my luck is going to change."

I was aware of Lorraine losing her voice. She began to pace back and forth behind me as though she couldn't

bear to look at what was going on at the table. I think
what happened was half her fault. She threw me off
balance; she confused me. She charged the whole place
with a lot of nervousness so I couldn't keep my mind on
the cards. You're supposed to play blackjack with Lady
Luck, not some girl who looks like she's ready for a
loony bin. She spoke to me only one more time, and
that was when I lost the five hundred and stuck a
thousand on my spot. I have to admit now that I was
going crazy. Suddenly chips didn't mean anything to
me anymore. I had to convert the money into chips
and it wasn't as though I was playing with money anymore, they were simply little round things. And the
whole idea wasn't cash, *it was winning*. I just *had* to
win. I couldn't lose. I'd had enough of losing in my life
and I didn't want to lose then, not there. Not in front of
all those people.

I could hear the music pouring out of the Calypso
Lounge. The band was playing a soft rhumba, and once
in a while I would look up from the chips and see Dolly
and the Colonel swaying to and fro across the floor. The
chips began to run through my fingers like water. I was
going down, and there off in the lounge was this thin,
tired, frail old man keeping pace with Dolly Racinski
every step of the way. They were having such a good
time, it only made me feel even more guilty as I lost
and lost again. I made larger and larger bets. I tried
making smaller bets. I tried skipping a hand. Lorraine
began to moan. Lorraine tried literally pulling me away
from the table. Finally, I stopped playing. The money
was all gone, and Lorraine was in tears. And then I
realized how really off the deep end I had gone. I asked
Lorraine if she would lend me the few bucks she had
left. And she just stood there, her tears freezing on her
face. Now she was completely mute.

The last thing I was aware of was the music roaring
from the Calypso Lounge: "*Hold that tiger. Hold that
tiger.*" I felt my own eyes clouding over with moisture
and shame. I looked up to see Dolly and the Colonel
again. They were gliding across the dance floor doing
these tiny steps that made their feet appear to be
inches off the ground. It was something like a dance

97

I've seen old people do called The Peabody. Sometimes the music would pause, and the Colonel would spin Dolly around and do a big dip. How could I tell them that I'd lost everything? How could I tell them?

Twelve

I couldn't look John in the face. I was beyond anger. I was horrified. He just wouldn't listen to me. I wanted to run out the door and not even look back. I just wanted to get on a bus and not have to face him, or anyone. He had taken the Colonel's life into his own hands and lost it playing cards. He had not only tried to act like some kind of professional gambler, he had tried to act like God. Maybe I was just as guilty. It seemed we had a habit of stepping in and taking control of other people's lives. It was only when I saw that the shame was so unbearable for John that he couldn't lift his eyes up from the floor that I began to feel sorry for him.

"You've got to tell them," I said. "You've got to tell them *now.*"

"I can't," John said.

"You've got to," I demanded. I took his hand and pulled him away from the blackjack tables through the crowd. I dragged him right into the Calypso Lounge and stood him in front of Dolly and the Colonel at their table.

"*Tell them,*" I ordered John.

When he didn't speak, I just blurted it out. "He's lost all your money," I said. "He's lost over four thousand dollars."

Dolly's mouth dropped open. You could tell she didn't really believe it. It was some little joke the kids were playing. That's what she must have thought. The old man didn't say anything, but Dolly's eyes kept scattering looks all over the place like she expected to hear some voice tell her this was a joke and the money was indeed still in John's pocket.

"I mean it," I said to Dolly. "He lost it. He lost it *all.*"

"It's true," John said in a voice so low you could

hardly hear it over the band, which was now playing "Good Night, Sweetheart."

Dolly stood up and put her hands on John's shoulders. John lifted his head and looked at her.

"You lost all the money?" Dolly asked.

John nodded.

"Oh, John, I'm so ashamed," I cried, and now I couldn't help putting my arms around him and burying my head in his shoulder. I started to cry uncontrollably. And for a long time John and I couldn't say a word. Then Dolly did something very strange. She moved us away from the Colonel's table and whispered to us, "It's all right. Don't worry about it."

I looked at her amazed. "What do you mean, *it's all right?*"

"Just forget it," Dolly said. "Forget it ever happened."

"How can I?" John asked.

"Please believe me when I say *it really doesn't matter*," Dolly emphasized, tilting her head to one side so her pom-pom earrings cast a halo around her head. And that was all Dolly or the Colonel had to say. The Colonel stood up, looking very sad, and the four of us moved through the crowd to the doors and outside. The air from the sea now seemed cold and chilling. And the length of the Boardwalk from where we had started seemed enormous. Suddenly all the modes of transportation were very crowded. It seemed like everyone was leaving at once, like rats deserting a ship. We all managed to get on the geriatric perambulator when it finally stopped in front of us, because none of us had the energy to walk at all. Midway down the Boardwalk the contraption broke down, and a lot of the old ladies riding on it began to make nasty comments to the driver. Some were letting off high-frequency cackles about how they had to get back to their hotels to rest up. It was depressing to hear them. We sat there for over forty minutes waiting until the next contraption came along, and we were transferred into it.

From that point on everything got even blacker. The valet brought us the Studebaker and it wouldn't budge after we got inside. The retarded valet had stepped on the emergency brake so heavily that we couldn't release it until John inverted himself under the dashboard and yanked around at some wires and springs. Finally the brake released, cutting into John's thumb and drawing blood. I wanted to give him my handkerchief, but he refused it as though he wasn't worthy of it. All I wanted to do now was to get out of Atlantic City and go home. There seemed to be some kind of force that was holding us back, making us stay to remind us about the terrible thing we had done to this poor miserable man. As we drove down Atlantic Avenue, Dolly reached forward and gave me a Band-Aid she had in her doghouse pocketbook for John's thumb. I put it on as we passed the bull mural outside the Ramada Inn, and I couldn't help thinking how old Taurus had won. He had gored us good and strong, flung us into the air on his horns. Then we hit the Garden State Parkway and raced northward.

"We're sorry Colonel," I finally managed to say, turning around.

"Don't worry about it," Dolly spoke up. "Everything that happened was my fault," she insisted. "This was my idea. The Colonel wanted a day out, and I picked Atlantic City because I saw it in all the television advertisements. I thought it was glamorous and fun, and we'd all have a good time. I'm just a foolish old lady who should stick to pushing garbage around with my broom."

"You're not foolish," the Colonel said. "You're not foolish at all. If it hadn't been for you, I'd still be trapped in that house, and tomorrow, who knows? I had more fun today than I ever had in my life. I don't have any regrets. We tried, and that's the important thing. It's the people in this world who never try who go to their grave full of regrets. You're a wonderful woman, Dolly, and don't you ever forget that. And what's the big deal about the silver dollars? I only kept them because they were old. I didn't know they were worth money. I had a good time, and I don't want you kids looking like you just lost your best friend."

"We can't just forget it," I said. "John and I will make it up to you. We'll come every day. We'll clean up the house. We'll bring you food. We'll do it for five years or as long as it takes to pay you back."

"You don't have to," the Colonel said, and then he turned back to Dolly. He let go of her hand and reached up and took the gold chain and crystal fossil from around his neck. "I want you to have this, Dolly. I want you to wear this and always think of me." He placed it around Dolly's neck. For the first time we saw Dolly at a loss for words. She just stared at her lap holding on to the Colonel's hands. The fumes from the Jersey refineries smacked us in our faces, and they smelled like death. You could feel the poison pouring into your lungs. I remembered reading an article about how even the deer in New Jersey were showing up with cancers. I got so depressed, I felt that not only John and I had gone down the tubes, but Dolly, the Colonel, and the entire world, the entire money-grubbing world had allowed all the horrible chimneys to spit their pollution into the air and slowly infect and kill everything for hundreds of miles around. But what I really couldn't figure out is that we had really failed the Colonel—but he had forgiven us! I just couldn't understand how Dolly and the Colonel could forgive us. Then John stepped on the gas and took the Studebaker up to her full speed.

"Oh, I feel like a girl again," Dolly said, touching the fossil around her neck and kissing the Colonel's hand. Suddenly though I noticed the Colonel look like he was really going downhill. There seemed to be an awful amount of sweat pouring down his face.

"What's the matter?" Dolly wanted to know.

"I just had a dream, but I'm wide awake."

"That's called a *daydream*." Dolly tried to smile.

"I had this vision," the old man slowly said, "that I was being nailed inside of a coffin. My feet and arms and legs were immobile. There was nothing I could do to get out of it."

Dolly took the Colonel's arm and held him tightly. "I'm here, Colonel, and I won't be going away. I'll stay with you." Again I had the feeling they were sharing a secret.

Now I began to feel ashamed for a different reason. I

was ashamed because I could see that Dolly was being very supportive of the Colonel at a time when he needed it, while I was doing nothing for John. I was suffering in my own shame, worried about myself when I should have been able to reach out and do something to help him. I could see in John's eyes as they froze ahead on the highway that he was dying a thousand deaths. Just even looking at him, caring to notice him, seemed a step in the right direction. I looked behind and saw Dolly clutching the Colonel, comforting him. I remembered what I had learned from all the best psychological journals, we are what we *do*, not what we *say*. It took all the guts in the world I had to reach out and put my hand on John's arm. He still couldn't look at me, but just touching him told me what I had to do. I moved next to him and I put my arm around him. And for some reason I kissed his neck. John looked at me for a moment and I could tell I had done the right thing. I could tell he felt, at least for a moment, that he had some worth. That he still was a pretty terrific guy and that I was going to forgive him for what really was a sickness. I always knew that gambling was a sickness, and somehow I felt that without even speaking at this moment, even John realized it was the same as being a drunk. The force that had come over him and made him throw all that money away was no doubt the same kind of force that had made his father an alcoholic. There's not much difference between not being able to say no to a pair of dice or a pack of cards and not being able to say no to a martini.

Then I did something I never thought I'd have the nerve to do. I reached my right hand across to his face and stroked his cheek gently. There was no way he could think I was doing it just as a friend. He kept his eyes glued on the road ahead, as he had to. Somehow at this very moment, I needed him to know that I loved him fully, totally, *desperately*—and that I not only forgave him, but would stay with him until the end of the universe and the death of infinity.

After a while I checked on Dolly and the Colonel in the rearview mirror. They were hypnotized by each other. I watched as the Colonel took Dolly's hand in his and I heard him speaking over the din of the motor: "My life has always been my work. I've never loved a woman, but now I see all that I have missed." He kissed Dolly's hand, and she beamed as though she were the Queen of the Stardust Ballroom.

By the time we were crossing the bridge back onto Staten Island, Dolly was speaking about the future. If it was up to her, she said, she would like to see the town house, to share all the memories the Colonel had stored there. She thought his blue-prints and plans should be donated to some engineering institute so they could be put on display and used as reference for all the young people coming along. We shot along like a yellow comet. We had just passed Todt Hill Road when I couldn't help noticing the Colonel's face looked as though he was in some discomfort. I thought maybe I was seeing things. But a few moments after that I was aware of the fact that beads of sweat were beginning to form on his temple. I could see that John had finally noticed in the rearview mirror. But Dolly was too busy talking to see. I turned around to look at the Colonel and I could see even his breathing had changed. He was taking in deep breaths of air, obviously not even listening to Dolly anymore. I tried to hold back from letting John know how afraid I was, because I didn't want to make him any more anxious than he was. I had sensed something awful was going to happen. And when I heard the Colonel's voice, I knew he was really in trouble this time.

"Oh, God, the pain . . . the pain. . . . Oh, God . . ." The words came out of the Colonel's mouth and lingered in our ears for just a moment and then were replaced by a cry of anguish which could only belong to a dying man.

Thirteen

If it hadn't been for Dolly, Lorraine and I would have just collapsed. We hadn't heard cries like those that came out of the Colonel since our Pigman had died of a heart attack right in front of us. Dolly took complete charge. She made me keep driving beyond the Pigman's house and go directly to Staten Island Hospital. She got the attendants at the emergency room to put the old man on a stretcher and roll him directly past Admissions into an examination room. Within minutes a doctor was hovering over the old guy and Dolly said a few quick words. She knew all the right information, and before the blood could come back into Lorraine's and my faces, the old man was being rolled up to an intensive-care floor. Lorraine and I stood mute and helpless, and we were so grateful for having an adult help us for a change. I guess we sensed the limitations of being a kid when the chips were down.

Before Dolly went up with the Colonel, she came to us in the hall and leveled with us.

"He's going to die," she said. "He knew he only had a few weeks to live anyway, which is why he ran away from the town house. He wanted to die on his own and not in a poorhouse."

"You knew this?" I managed to ask.

"He told me the first night I met him," Dolly said. "He had been cut open several times before that when surgeons tried to patch him up. The last time all they could do was sew him back up and tell him to get his affairs in order. He loves you," Dolly said. "He loves you because you saved him from being alone in his last days."

"Will we see him again?" Lorraine asked.

Dolly looked very depressed. "I think we should all go up now and see if we can say good-bye."

She walked quickly to the elevators, Lorraine and I scurrying to keep up with her. We got into one of the elevators. It was huge, designed to carry stretchers and X-ray machines and stuff like that. The one we got in had a couple of sad-looking visitors, a doctor who obviously thought he was hot stuff, and two nurses balancing plasma jars attached to an old lady patient who looked like she was going to croak any minute. The old lady had all kinds of needles in her and a tube up her nose. She looked at us as though she wanted to say, "Oh, my poor kids, life is so painful I feel sorry for what lies ahead for you."

The lights indicating the different floors of the hospital lit up as we rose in the air: NURSERY, CARDIOLOGY, PEDIATRICS, etc. Finally we got off at the intensive-care ward. Dolly seemed to sense exactly where to go. She didn't even have to inquire at the nurses' station. In a moment we were outside a room where there was a lot of activity. We could glimpse inside, where the Colonel was being lowered onto a bed. One nurse was pressing a button thing on the end of a cord that lowered the head of the bed. Another nurse was shoving a needle into the Colonel's arm and attaching it to a hanging bag of clear fluid. Still another was attaching electrodes to his body and taking readings. A doctor gave him an injection of something and was talking so quietly we couldn't hear him from the doorway. At this point it seemed even Dolly didn't know what to do. A nurse came toward us saying, "You'll have to wait in the lounge. You'll have to wait in the lounge."

"I'm staying with him," Dolly said loud and clear.

"Are you his wife?" the nurse asked.

"I'm his girl friend," Dolly shot at her.

"Let her in here!" came a loud voice from the room. "Let her and my kids in here!" The Colonel had twisted his face to the side and practically yelled from the bed. The doctor had a stethoscope on the Colonel's heart and nodded *okay* to the nurse.

Dolly moved swiftly to the Colonel's side and took his hand. Lorraine and I couldn't budge from the doorway, almost afraid we'd use up too much of the oxygen in the room. Then an attendant barged past us rolling a

106

real oxygen tank with a water gauge and all. He banged it down on the floor to the right of the Colonel's bed. Dolly was saying soothing things to the Colonel like "Everything's going to be all right," which sort of counteracted all the other voices that were saying things like "Give him three milliliters," "What's his pulse?" and "Notify X-ray." All these people hovering over the Colonel when suddenly over it all came the Colonel's voice loud and clear:

"I want to marry her! I want to marry her!"

Everybody was shocked. Even Dolly.

"Get me a priest! Get a minister! I want to marry her!" the Colonel brayed.

"Later," Dolly whispered kindly.

"*Now!*" the Colonel demanded.

"Now is not the time to get married," the doctor said, loading another needle.

"Don't tell me what I want to do, you 3@#$%," the Colonel replied. Then he sat up in the bed and looked frantically for help. His eyes hit upon us at the doorway. "Get me a priest! Get me anybody!" he screamed at us.

"Yes, sir," I yelled back.

"*That's my boy!*" the Colonel practically cried. "*That's my boy!*"

I grabbed Lorraine's hand and dragged her all the way down the hall and into the elevator. It was empty except for some poor old lady in a Persian lamb coat who was simply crying by herself in the corner. Within two minutes Lorraine and I were in the Studebaker roaring out of the big oval in front of the hospital.

"Where are we going to get a priest?" Lorraine wanted to know.

"*Serendipity,*" I said, and it was the first time I had ever used the word in my life. I had first seen the word in an article about gambling, and it was supposed to mean something about being in the right place at the right time. I didn't really understand the whole meaning of it, but it meant that if you kept your eyes open the chances were pretty good that there had to be something that had been right in front of your eyes all the time and could solve almost any problem that ever

107

came up and you could win if you really wanted to be a winner. Even the Studebaker seemed to know where it was going as it exploded its way straight back up the road.

"If Dolly marries him and he dies, won't she have to pay all those tax bills?" Lorraine wanted to know.

"No," I said. "And even if she does, there'll be a lot left over after she sells the town house."

"The crocodile-skin room must be worth a lot, don't you think?"

"You bet," I agreed. "And don't forget his Keogh plan."

As we neared 190 Howard Avenue, I took my foot off the gas to let the motor quiet down. Sure enough, there was the sound of Gus barking away from within the house. In another moment we could see him at the front window, clawing away, looking very desperate—as though he knew something had happened to his master. But we weren't going to the house. We were going past it to the break in the huge hedges and down the driveway to the convent. I left Lorraine in the car with the motor running and dashed up the steps to the main entrance. I pressed the doorbell and banged on the front door until the nun who had been driving the tractor lawn mower appeared and opened up.

"I need a priest to marry somebody," I practically screamed.

"What's the rush?" she asked.

"The groom is eighty-two years old and dying," I said.

As if God himself had told her what was going on, she mumbled something about Father Santini, the resident priest, who lived in the garage apartment. I ran after her farther down the long driveway to the garage. She banged on a side door down the slope behind the garage and a very confused priest answered the door. I began shouting at him about this old man *who lived next door but who really was a runaway because the IRS had taken away his town house and he had broken in only to lick his wounds and die in peace—but he fell in love with a sixty-year-old custodial worker by the name of Dolly and he was dying now at Staten Island*

108

Hospital and wanted to marry her and could the priest come along this very minute before he croaked altogether from diverticulosis!

It turned out the priest was fresh over from Italy and could hardly understand English, much less everything I was pouring out to him. What he did understand was that he'd better come quick, and before you could say *Bingo!* we had a real live frocked priest in the backseat of the Studebaker with the top down and were roaring out of the convent. We were about to fly right past 190 Howard Avenue when I saw and heard Gus again, banging against the downstairs window, looking ready to throw himself through it. I knew a St. Bernard who did that one time and he broke the glass and got his neck caught on a jagged edge and died. I jammed on the brakes and told the priest I'd be right back. Lorraine was trying to explain the dog to him, and in a flash I was back with Gus and he jumped in the back right next to the priest and started licking him. It was a good thing the priest liked dogs.

The Studebaker made more noise than a Sherman tank as it cruised off the hill and back to the hospital. If you think everybody didn't look as we roared down Castleton Avenue and into the hospital oval, you're very much mistaken. We tried to get the priest and Gus into the hospital, but a guard at the front said we could only take the priest—so we had to put the top up and lock Gus up in the car with the windows open just a crack so he wouldn't suffocate. I knew it was only a temporary measure, so I didn't mind doing it to the poor dog—who you could just tell was salivating to see the Colonel.

Lorraine and I flanked the priest in the elevator to make sure he wouldn't get away from us. We watched the floors light up again as we ascended, NURSERY, CARDIOLOGY, etc. . . . . We erupted out of the thing on the intensive-care ward and rushed the priest straight to the Colonel's room. You never saw a more bedazzled collection of doctors and nurses than those there when we rammed this nice Italian priest right up to the side of the bed. The Colonel's face ignited with joy.

"I want to marry her *now!*" the Colonel demanded,

pointing at Dolly, who was holding his hand. It took another couple of minutes before it all sank in. Dolly did some double-talk and pleaded for the Colonel to wait, but the Colonel knew he didn't have time for any waiting. The Colonel said Lorraine and I could be the witnesses, but the priest said we weren't old enough. By now the medical profession was getting into the swing of things and a nurse and an attendant agreed to stand up for the nuptial ceremony.

"Hurry, will you?" the Colonel brayed.

The priest took out a little prayer book of some kind and started talking in broken English. The look of peace that fell over the Colonel's face as he listened to the words was something I'll never forget. It was a look so beautiful and yet deadly: I knew the Colonel was getting ready to die in peace. And then I did something instinctive. I knew there was only one more thing I could do for him. I grabbed Lorraine's hand and started running down the hall with her. It was almost religious the way she seemed to know there was just one thing left that we had to make happen. We jumped into the elevator and started back down toward the ground floor. The thoughts that ran through my mind were like a tapestry, complicated, *embroidered* in my brain. My mind skipped from one thread to another, and I could tell Lorraine's brain was doing the same thing. It was like a series of little pictures—*Dolly dancing with the Colonel at the Calypso Lounge. Her earrings shining above her lips, her always saying "Lookin' up. Lookin' up!" Lorraine's voice in the bedroom of the town house: "No woman ever lived here." The acidophilus milk. The Game of Life, with the Wall of Death at the end of it. The Cup of Love and the fossil swinging around the Colonel's neck. "When it comes time to die, you will fight it," I remembered the Colonel telling me, but I realized he was really telling me about himself. "You will struggle, and you will claw at it. You will do everything possible to escape it!"*

When we reached the Studebaker it was as though the dog was screaming at us—"Hurry! Hurry, you teenage jerks!" We yanked open the door and Gus ran beside us. Lorraine, Gus, and I ran straight in the front door past the outraged guard. "Hey, stop! Stop!" the guy yelled, but we didn't. We reached the elevator, but the guard was fast behind us.

"Here!" I called, and pushed open a door that said *Staircase*.

The dog ran faster up the stairs than we could. It seemed like Gus knew right where he was going. He was waiting, whining at the top of the fifth-floor stairwell, and I pulled the door open for him. The three of us galloped past the nurses' station. Past a dozen rooms, and Gus' hind legs almost skidded out from under he as he veered into the Colonel's room.

"He's dead, my darlings," Dolly sobbed, rushing into our arms. "My darling's dead."

Gus jumped up onto the bed, almost knocking over the doctor, and started licking the poor Colonel's face. If there's a God in heaven or anywhere I just know the Colonel must have felt those kisses as he traveled deeper into his Death.

Fourteen

John and Dolly had to hold me up as I burst into tears and I felt my legs going out from under me. I heard the doctor tell John to get me some air, and once I got outside the hospital room I was able to walk.

"I'm his wife," Dolly told us. "*I'm his wife*. I've got to sign some papers and take care of calling a funeral director." She stayed with us in the hall until she was certain I wouldn't faint. We could hear Gus whining inside. It was such a sad whimpering.

"He's on the bed with him," Dolly said, tears flooding down her face though she stood tall and strong. "Gus knows the Colonel is dead."

"We'll take him," John said.

"You just get Lorraine to the car and wait for us," Dolly suggested. "It may take a little while, but we'll be down. I want Gus to stay with me. He'll stay with me from now on."

"You bet," John agreed. "You sure you're okay?"

Dolly nodded affirmatively. "You kids are swell. You kids are just swell." She managed to smile.

As we walked away from the room, we could hear the priest giving last rites in Italian or something. Near the elevator I thought my legs were going to give out on me again, but John held me until I felt my strength come back.

"Breathe deeply," he kept repeating. "*Breathe deeply*." After a few minutes I was ready to get on the elevator. I felt so confused, and in a strange way embarrassed. I was leaning too much on John. I was being too weak—almost as if I had been *trained* to be weak. Somewhere inside me I felt the voice of my mother telling me I was weak, that I was supposed to be weak. That *all women were weak*, which is why they had to watch out for boys who were strong and could control girls and do whatever they wanted to them. I tried to be strong, to stop the helplessness I was feeling, and my first act was to reach out myself and press the button on the elevator for the ground floor. At least I thought I had pressed for the ground floor, but the elevator came to a stop on the second and the door opened to reveal a wall of glass. I heard the sounds of babies crying, and as the elevator door started to close again I shot my foot forward and stopped the door. For some reason I just wanted to get off, and it didn't take John long to adapt to the unusual. I fought now to halt my crying, and my eyes surveyed the wall of glass in front of us. This was not an endless wall but more like a picture window. I let go of John's hand and walked forward as though I was viewing a huge mural in a museum. When I reached the edge of the glass, I felt John's hands slipping around my waist and we both looked into the glass room. What met our eyes were about two dozen tiny babies, and it seemed they were all looking up at us from white boatlike cradles. They each had a card on the front of their bassinets—even the few that were only inches long and wiggling in incubators. The biggest baby was a Chinese one with a full head of hair. Its card said, "GLORIA WONG, 10 pounds 5 ounces, born May 21, 8:04 A.M."

My eyes traveled over the cards. There was a JOHNNIE and a SEAN and a LUCILLE and a HELEN, and they were so cute I wanted to reach out and touch them all. Two nurses were busy inside the glass room changing and feeding these new arrivals to our world—and I felt like I was watching a pair of lovely gardeners tending the most beautiful crop the world could grow. I was mesmerized, being drawn back through time and up into the highest, most brilliant galaxies. I felt as though I was in a dream and that John was flying with me, hurtling toward the very center of Life itself. I was drugged, desperately standing in a field of simple, priceless flowers, when I heard John's voice whisper in my ear.

"*I want to spend my life with you,*" John said so gently and sincerely my entire body heard. We turned toward each other, holding on to one another there in front of that glass wall that I felt held the answer to every mystery of what we were doing on this earth to begin with. Our bodies were touching and there was no shame, there was no fear, there was no Death.

Love.

That was our legacy—the gift which had come to us through our Pigman.

Our legacy was *love*.

ABOUT THE AUTHOR

Paul Zindel was born and raised on Staten Island, New York, and currently lives in Manhattan. He is the author of several novels for young adults, a picture book, theater plays, and numerous screenplays. His first two novels, *The Pigman* and *My Darling, My Hamburger*, were selected as Outstanding Books of the Year by *The New York Times*, and *The Effect of Gamma Rays on Man-in-the-Moon Marigolds* won the 1971 Pulitzer Prize for Drama and the New York Critics Circle Award.

Paul Zindel enjoys television, movies, dream interpretation, swimming, and fattening foods—particularly Hunan cuisine and ice cream. He also likes new experiences and teenagers who need someone to confide in.